DAVE AND GEORGIA

AND OTHER STORIES

DAVE AND GEORGIA
AND OTHER STORIES

TOM LARMORE

Charleston, SC
www.PalmettoPublishing.com

Dave and Georgia
And Other Stories
Copyright © 2022 by Tom Larmore

First Edition

Hardcover ISBN: 979-8-8229-0049-3
Paperback ISBN: 979-8-8229-0050-9
eBook ISBN: 979-8-8229-0051-6

Dedication

To Valerie, who listened.

TABLE OF CONTENTS

Spacers 169

Annie the Sex Robot 181

An Ordinary Man 207

About the Author 225

DAVE

—=AND=—

GEORGIA

CHAPTER ONE

―――――――●――――――

THE WOMAN IN GREEN

In the grassy field, the woman in green picked a white flower.

In that moment, I fell in love with her.

I prayed to God, "Let her be mine."

God said to me: "If you want her, go talk to her."

I said: "I will."

I walked up to the woman in green.

She turned, her red hair flowing, and said to me, "Oh, a man. How do you do?"

"I was fine," I said, "until I saw you. Now, my heart is filled with wanting something I can't have."

"What is it?" she asked. "That you can't have?"

"You."

She smiled. "Whoever told you, I was something you can't have?"

I smiled back. "Would you like some coffee?"

"I would love some coffee," she said.

That was the beginning.

CHAPTER TWO

DAVE

At work, all they talked about was the war.

At lunch, in the cafe, all they talked about was the war.

After work, I went home. She was waiting for me with dinner. She wanted to talk about the war.

"You promised," I said, sitting down at the table. "We wouldn't talk about it."

She put a Weave sheet in front of me.

"They've invaded Alossi," she said, panic in her voice. "That's only one Gate away."

"You promised," I repeated, helping myself to some meat. "We wouldn't talk about it."

"We have to talk about it, Dave," she said. "This came for you today."

She handed me a brown envelope. "It's from the government," she said. "Sent certified, to make sure there was a record you got it."

I took a knife, opened the envelope, and pulled out some papers. A letter, ordering me to report to the draft office, next Tuesday morning, at oh six hundred hours. Some forms, for me to fill out. Medical questions, mostly.

I put the papers back in the envelope, put it down on the table.

"Well?"

I said nothing. What could I say?

"Well?"

I composed my thoughts. "We knew, Georgia," I told her. "We knew this day would come. Now, please sit down, so we can eat dinner."

"Dave," she said, pacing around our tiny apartment. "What will we do?"

I didn't want to talk about it.

"Dave?"

"I will report to the draft office, like the letter says."

"What will *I* do?"

"You will do what wives do in times of war. Worry and wait. Pray that their husband returns."

"We could leave, Dave. To another world, far from the front."

"This world is our home, Georgia. Canassa is our home. We will stay."

"*I* will stay, Dave. You will be sent — God knows *where?*"

"It will be OK," I said. "The war will end and I will return."

Her eyes watered. "You don't know that, Dave. You could die."

I knew that. What did she want from me?

"Look," I said. "There's no point in talking about it. The draft letter came, I will report as ordered. End of discussion."

"Dave? Please — "

"End of discussion."

As ordered, I went to the draft office on Tuesday morning. I arrived at ten minutes before six. Hundreds of men were there, lined up outside.

I lit up a cigarette. The man behind me asked me for one, and as I lit it for him, we started talking.

"The Imperials are insane," he said. "Attacking the colonies, like *we're* the enemy."

I tried to keep my head clear of politics, but even I knew he didn't have his facts straight. "It's not the Empire attacking us, it's the Coalition."

"OK, right, I know that," he said. But he looked at me funny, and I knew he didn't know.

"The Coalition took over Earth," I told him, "after the Emperor died during the terrorist attack on Seven-Seven-Seven."

"Right," he said. "I understand." But clearly he didn't.

"The point is," I said. "The Coalition is run by people loyal to the Home Party. They're the guys who think all humans should return home to Earth. So, they're sending the Marines to each colony and forcing the colonists to return to Earth."

"But Canassa is my home," said the man. "I don't want to go back to Earth."

"Right," I told him. "All of us colonists feel that way. That's why there's a war."

He nodded, finally understanding.

The door of the draft office opened, and the line of men starting moving.

We were in a large room, hundreds of us. It looked like a high school basketball court, because that's what it was before the draft office took it over.

The man at the desk was in a brown military uniform. One by one, the men approached him, talked to him, then went beyond through a door. Finally, it was my turn. He didn't look up. "Name?"

"Dave Watson."

He reached into a file cabinet, pulled out a file, and opened it.

"Age — twenty-five," he said. Now he looked up. "Why are you here, Watson?"

"I was drafted."

"Why aren't you working in a factory?"

"I work at a book publisher. I illustrate children's books."

"Get an essential job, Watson. Then you won't get drafted. Get a job in a factory, making guns or bombs."

"I like my job."

"Here's the thing, Watson," said the man in uniform, looking annoyed. "We need eighteen-year-olds. At that age, men still think they're indestructible and will gladly follow orders to charge a machine gun nest. By the time a man reaches your age, he's wised up. He knows he can die, and that makes him cautious. Less useful to us. Do you understand?"

"I am here to do my duty for my world."

"Listen, Watson. Are you married?"

"Yes."

"Go home to your wife."

"I've been drafted. I intend to serve my world."

"Watson, I'm putting you down as 'medically unfit'. That way you won't be drafted again."

"I haven't had a physical. You can't say I'm 'medically unfit' unless a doctor examines me first."

The man in brown got angry. "Can't you see I'm doing you a favor, Watson? All the men in this room are going to die fighting the Impies. I'm letting you go, so you can go home to your wife and live."

"But —"

"Get the hell out, Watson."

"I —"

"M.P., please escort this man out."

A young man approached me. He had his hand on his holster.

"No need," I said. I walked towards the door.

I looked at the other men, realized they were all just boys. Destructible boys.

I hit the street, then went to work. I'd get an early start on my drawings.

CHAPTER THREE

GEORGIA

That night, Dave didn't want to talk about what happened at the draft office. He said they'd found him "medically unfit", but wouldn't give me details. I was curious, because I knew Dave was perfectly healthy. But he didn't want to talk about it, so I let it go.

Months went by, and the war went on. I kept up with the news updates, so I would know if we were in danger. Dave refused to listen if I ever tried to tell him what was going on. He seemed to think we were safe if he refused to think about it, but I knew otherwise.

One day, I realized I was late for my period. I took a pregnancy test. I was delighted to see a positive result. I told Dave when he got home from work.

His reaction was upsetting. "Bad time to have a baby."

I knew he was right, but I was angry. "What a horrible thing to say."

I thought we'd have a fight after I said that. A fight was long overdue. But he went into our bedroom and closed the door.

That Sunday, we went to Mass, as always. I didn't care that much about church, but Dave always insisted.

Most of the men were in uniform. Army. Navy. Orbit Guard. Home Guard. My husband was in civilian clothes.

The priest was giving a homily, saying that even in times of war, it was important to love our enemies.

"But God preserve our world from the godless Home Party and their unleashed dogs the Earth Marines," he said.

A young girl, fifteen maybe, came up to Dave and handed him a white feather. He looked at it with a dour expression.

The men in uniform stared. The women too.

I leaped at the girl and slapped her in the face. The sound echoed off the walls of the church.

Everyone froze. The priest stopped talking. The girl held her face and started to cry.

"How dare you give him that," I shouted. "He's 'medically unfit'. He wanted to fight, but they wouldn't take him."

There was a long silence, broken only by the girl's sobs.

"It's a lie," Dave said at last.

"What?" I cried.

"They didn't want me. They said I was too old."

"But you're not," I said.

"I know."

Dave put the feather in his shirt pocket and walked out. Not knowing what else to do, I followed him.

That night, there was a news flash. All nineteen of the agricultural worlds, Canassa included, had surrendered to the Coalition. The Earth Marines would be arriving on our world in thirteen days. We had that long to get out. If we stayed, we'd be forced to return to Earth.

"They put the colonists in death camps, Dave," I told my husband.

"I know, let me think."

"We're taking a ship to Artania," said my sister, Flo. "You should come with us."

"We don't have a lot of money," said Dave. "Just a few thousand. Not enough to get to Artania."

"They're letting people go without paying and letting them work off the debt," said Jim, Flo's husband.

"Indentured servitude," said Dave. "No, thank you."

"It's better than a death camp," I said. "It's not just us anymore, Dave. We have to think about the baby."

I thought we'd fight, then. I wanted to fight, it would be good for our marriage.

But he said, "You're right, Georgia. We will go to Artania."

It was a colony transport, big enough to carry one million humans in cold storage, another fifty thousand warm. They sent Jim, Flo and Dave down below to get frozen, told me to go forward to the women's dorm.

"I want to be with my husband," I said.

"We don't put pregnant women in hibernation," said the Artanian woman, dressed in white. "Please move along, there's a lot of people coming after you and we have to leave in less than an hour."

"Move it lady," said a woman's voice from behind me. I felt a shove.

I turned around with my fist clenched, but saw she was holding a small child.

The Artanian grabbed me then, shoved me towards the door, then shoved the woman with the child too. "We don't freeze children either," she said in a manner of explanation.

I walked the long way to the women's dorm, the woman and child behind me. There were thousands of women there, and just as many children. The bunks were stacked four high in a room as large as a football field.

"It stinks," said the child.

It did. Many of these women had already spent a week in this room, without baths or showers. An Artanian in white greeted us with another shove towards the bunks and a firm instruction to strap ourselves in.

"The Earthies have arrived in system," said a man's voice on the intercom. "Strap down. We'll be leaving immediately."

He wasn't kidding. The entire room shifted, and I fell to the deck, and so did the woman with the child.

"The captain said to strap down," yelled the woman in white. She didn't wait for us to respond. She grabbed the child, strapped it down to a bunk and then grabbed the woman and strapped her down too. I didn't wait to be manhandled, I found a bunk and strapped myself down.

"How long is the trip to Artania?" I asked.

"Eight weeks," said the Artanian. "Unless the Earthies are blocking the Gate. If that happens, we'll have to take the long way around."

Misery, that's all I can say about the trip to Artania.

The Artanians had done the best they could. Every military and civilian ship that could be spared had been sent to the agricultural colonies to evacuate as many humans as possible. But the fleet had been quickly assembled, and there hadn't been time to stock the ships with adequate provisions.

So food was tightly rationed. The children had enough, but the adults went hungry. We all lost weight, and some of the older women died. I had always been pleasingly plump, as Dave said, but after the trip to Artania, I was always thin and had to struggle to keep the weight on.

The Artanians didn't allow us out of the women's dorm, except to use the head and showers, and then we were escorted by armed guards. It was like they didn't trust us. Also, I began to realize that Artanians believed they were humanity's elite, and looked down on us agricultural colonists. It showed in the snobby way even the lowest ranked crew member treated us.

Religion was also an issue. We colonists were mostly Catholics. The Artanians were mostly Humanists. I heard one Artanian crew member tell another that the Pope might show up on Artania and start bossing people around. Roberta, the woman who had shoved me, stopped me before I could give the Artanian woman a knuckle sandwich.

"You'll end up in the brig," she said. "On a diet of bread and water."

"They wouldn't do that, I'm pregnant."

"Do you want to take the chance? You have to think about the baby."

That night, I wished again that Dave were with me.

But I thanked my lucky stars that at least he wasn't a soldier, off somewhere fighting in this horrible war.

CHAPTER FOUR

———— ◖ ————

DAVE

Normally, they give people taken out of cold storage a full twenty-four hours of bed rest to recover. We refugees from Canassa were hustled off the ship within minutes after thaw and herded like cattle out the airlock. After a good deal of pushing and shoving, I found myself in an open enclosure surrounded by one million packed in humans. There wasn't even room to sit down.

All I could think, was: *Where's Georgia?*

My data-com had been taken away before I was put on ice, so there was no way to call her.

"Oh God," I said to God. "What if I never find Georgia?"

"You will find her," God told me. "That's not the real problem."

"What's the real problem?"

God chose that moment not to talk to me. But then, I figured out the problem for myself. There was snow on the ground, and the temperature was barely above freezing. And I was not dressed for it.

I looked around. Almost no one was dressed for it.

"Jesus," a man nearby yelled. "Are they going to let us all die out here in the cold after hauling us through four Gates? They're just going to let us die?"

"I thought the Artanians had weather control?" said one woman, holding twin girls close in her arms. Both of them were turning blue and trembling. "Why the hell are they allowing us to freeze?"

Drones were floating overhead, stopping in front of each of us for a moment and moving on.

"They're screening us," said a man wearing a winter overcoat. He seemed to be the only one dressed appropriately. "They're making sure we're not Home Party."

"What's wrong with being Home Party?" said a small man in spectacles who looked like a professor.

"Where the hell have you been, pal?" said the first man. "We're at war with the Home Party."

"We're at war with the Coalition," said the professor. "There is nothing illegal about being a member of the Home Party so long as you obey the law."

The crowd parted and a hulking chrome-covered war robot towered over the professor. "You will come with me, sir."

"What? What if I refuse to come with you?"

The robot didn't argue, but grabbed the small man, picked him up, and carried him away.

"I'm a citizen of the Empire," he shouted. "I have rights."

I looked in every direction and saw robots hauling people off. I had a feeling I'd never see any of them again.

Aerial vehicles approached, each with a large metallic object slung underneath. In a pattern, they hovered down towards us. A monotone voice said, "Clear the area. Clear the area. Clear the area."

We parted, pushing and shoving, and the vehicles dropped off their cargoes. Immediately after unloading, the objects activated, radiating heat. We huddled around to warm ourselves. At least now, we wouldn't freeze to death. But, we might starve.

Small plastic packages dropped from the sky by the thousands. I picked one up, looked at the label: "Beef Stew." I decided to grab as many as I could, but other people were thinking the same thing. It became a free-for-all. One man punched another man in the mouth and took his packages. But after a few moments, calmer heads prevailed and the violence stopped.

I had three packages, so I wouldn't starve today.

———————

We had come to Artania to avoid death camps but had ended up in a camp just the same. They assigned the men to low bunkhouses, one hundred to each. It was warm, we were fed, but we were severely restricted in our movements. Armed robots guarded the grounds. Four days after I had arrived, it was my turn to be "processed."

I was led to a bare room with white walls, with only a table and two chairs. A man in a white uniform sat across me. He was not even attempting to look friendly. He had a tri-vi computer screen in front of him. He did not look up.

"Name?"

He already knew the answer. My bio sheet was displayed on the tri-vi image.

"Dave Watson."

"Dave, how interesting. Not short for 'David'. Your parents named you 'Dave.'"

I said nothing.

"Date of birth?"

"May 2, 2984."

"Home world?"

"You know my home world. You just took me from there."

"Home world?"

"Canassa."

"Profession?"

"I illustrate children's books."

He looked at me. "Any book I might have read? I have three children myself."

He already knew the answer. He was trying to play me, but I saw through his game.

"*The Lonely Scout*, it's a best seller."

"That's on the Home Party's list of banned books."

"I am aware." This had hurt sales, which meant less in royalties for me. Not that I was getting much in the first place.

"Do you agree with the message of the book?"

I was alert. Felt I might be in danger.

"What message? It's a children's book."

"Indeed, children's books can be very effective propaganda. You must be aware of that, Mr. Watson."

I was cautious. "I never thought of it that way."

"*The Lonely Scout* is about a scout ship who travels further and further from Earth. He is lonely, and gets lonelier. But in the end, he realizes its worth it because he's helping the human race expand to the stars."

"Yes, that's the gist of it."

The man in white seemed pleased.

"Do you have a job lined up after you're released?"

"I assumed I'd be an indentured servant."

The man looked irritated. "You assumed we Artanians own slaves? How could you possibly think that?"

"How else do we pay back the debt from our journey here?"

"There is no debt. But if you want to work, I think I know a good place for you."

"If I want to work? Of course I want to work."

"Good," said the man. He pushed a few buttons. "Normally, there'd be a battery of questions to make sure you are politically reliable. But I think the illustrator of *The Lonely Scout* qualifies for 'AAA Loyalty Status'. What do you think, Mr. Watson?"

I could see on the tri-vi image that my face had just been covered with the letters 'AAA'.

I hoped this was good news.

I realized later the whole interview had been a set up. Him pretending he didn't know who I was, was an act. They knew I was coming the moment I set foot on the colony ship.

CHAPTER FIVE

―――――――●―――――――

GEORGIA

I won't tell you all the details of my experiences at the camp. But I will say this: with the shortage of food, the cold, and all the health hazards of living in tight quarters with hundreds of other women, I lost the baby. So, add grief to all my other miseries.

I was surprised when I was interviewed, after it was determined I was not a Home Party loyalist, when the woman asking the questions said, "On behalf of her majesty's government, you have our condolences for the loss of your unborn child. However, in this case, there's something we can to mitigate your loss."

The door of the room opened, and a woman in a brown uniform led in a little girl. She had sad eyes. She looked hungry and tired.

"Her name is Raine. Her parents died during the Battle of Alene. We are assigning her to you and your husband to foster."

"What?" I asked. "Don't we get a choice?"

The woman looked at me briefly, then went back to her computer tri-vi image.

"No, you have no choice," she said. "But your basic income will be adjusted accordingly, and you will be assigned a larger apartment."

"Can I at least consult with my husband? He may not want to foster a child."

The woman stopped what she was doing and looked at me.

"I understand your reluctance to take on such a large responsibility, Mrs. Watson," she said. "But the Queen's government has done a lot for you, saving you from Earth forces and bringing you here. Now, it's time for you to do something for us. We're in the second year of a war with the Coalition, and with the surrender of the agricultural worlds, Artania stands alone. Population-wise, we're outnumbered almost twenty to one. We're not asking you to join the military and fight. All we're asking is that you take on one orphan. Can you do that, Mrs. Watson?"

I looked at the girl. Her eyes pleaded with me. I knew enough about orphanages to realize she'd had it tough.

"I will take her."

"Good, Mrs. Watson," said the woman. "Take these forms and report to the next station. There, you will be given your family's identity cards, your basic income cards, your ration cards, your new data-coms, and the keys to your apartment and ground car."

"An apartment and ground car? Do we pay for these?"

"No."

"How is this possible?"

"You are used to the pure capitalism of the agricultural colonies. Here on Artania, our system is a bit different."

I wanted to ask questions, but the woman's attitude made it clear she was in a hurry. But I had to ask:

"When will I see my husband?"

"Soon, Mrs. Watson. Families will be reunited at the end of the process."

"Uh, thanks?"

"Don't thank me, Mrs. Watson. I'm just doing my job. Next!"

Dave looked sick and he nearly collapsed in my arms when I ran over and hugged him, Raine in tow.

"Oh my God, Dave, you look like a malaria victim."

"It's the after-effect of hibernation," he said. "It will wear off. I just need to lie down."

We were in a starship hanger, set up as the family re-unification room slash morgue. Half of the hanger was full of refugees, greeting each other, laughing with joy, despite the cold, the hunger, the pain of losing loved ones. One quarter of the hanger was full of our luggage, and refugees were matching tags and claiming pieces as they found them. The final quarter of the hanger was filled with coffins, thousands of them, each draped with the Artanian flag. I made up my mind not to let the sight upset me.

"Who's the girl?" Dave wanted to know.

"Our new foster daughter," I said, hoping for a good response.

It was not forthcoming. "Just what we need, another mouth to feed," he said.

Raine heard, and I saw her face fall.

I wanted to start a fight with Dave, tell him off, but this was not the time.

Our new apartment was in a well-off sector of Central City, not a rat hole in a slum as I'd expected would be assigned to a refugee family. It was spacious, much larger than the tiny apartment we'd had on Canassa. The heater turned on automatically as soon as we entered, and within minutes the cold outside was nearly forgotten. I checked the kitchen, found it equipped with modern appliances. The living room had an entertainment center with tri-vi and stereo. We were on a high elevation level, with an excellent view. To the East were the spires of the Queen's Palace. Beyond that the dome of the Parliament Building.

We looked in the bedrooms, they were spacious as well.

All the rooms were fully furnished, and Raine's room was decorated with pink wallpaper and carpet, and full of dolls and stuffed animals. Her eyes lit up with joy.

She still had not said a word to me.

"How did we rate this luxury?" I asked Dave.

"I've been given a new job in the Propaganda Department."

"Is that what they call it? The 'Propaganda Department'?"

"That's what it is. They call it the 'Ministry of Culture' but the job I'm assigned is to use my artistic talent to whip up enthusiasm for the war."

He was angry, I could see it in the way his nostrils flared.

"Well, Dave, is that so bad?" I hoped I could calm him down. I was sure the apartment was bugged, and it would not be good if our hosts believed Dave was anything but Jumping through the Gate for his new job.

"You know I hate politics, Georgia," said Dave. "And I hate the war. I was willing to fight as a soldier and die for my world. But this is different. I'd be getting my hands dirty telling lies so boys will gladly join up to be laser fodder."

Would this be a good time to start a fight? I had felt for at least a year that the main problem in our marriage was we didn't fight, leaving so many issues unresolved. Every time I tried to start a fight, Dave would simply leave the room. Things needed to be aired between us, and that required a fight. But, I realized, this was not the time. "When do you start?"

"Monday."

"OK, here's the thing," I said. "Don't jump to any conclusions about your new job, promise? Go in with an open mind. Maybe it won't be so bad. OK?"

Dave shrugged, then went to the refrigerator and pulled out a beer.

Then he sat down, put on a tri-vi show and started to watch it.

I realized, he wasn't going to respond to what I had said.

Raine watched us, looking first at me, then at Dave. Her eyes were sad, but sharp, intelligent, like she understood exactly what was happening between me and Dave, and feeling unsafe because of it.

"Come on, Raine," I said, reaching out and taking her hand. "Both of us need a bath."

The refrigerator was state-of-the art, but its shelves were nearly bare. I went to the underground garage, put Raine in her car seat, and took the ground car to the supermarket to restock on food.

The supermarket was larger than any I'd ever seen, the size of a starship hanger and four stories high. Robots hustled around, polishing the floor and keeping everything sparkly clean. But there was a lot of emptiness. I saw a well-stocked meat department, but everything else was in short supply. I stopped a robot in its tracks, and asked: "Where's all the food?"

The robot, a shiny white model with a feminine form, seemed embarrassed. "I'm afraid, ma'am, due to wartime conditions —"

"Did you call me 'ma'am?'"

Believe it or not, after all the suffering I'd been through, this was my main concern — that a robot had called me "ma'am."

"I'm sorry 'missus?'"

"People have always called me 'miss' before. Why did you call me 'ma'am?'"

"Miss, I assure you that I meant no disrespect. I will, of course, refer to you by you preferred title of 'miss.'"

"Just answer the question, robot. Why did you call me 'ma'am.'"

"I suppose it was the presence of the child, miss. You are the girl's mother?"

Raine was five years old. To be her mother, I would have to be at least twenty-three. But I was twenty, not even old enough to go into a bar and order a drink. With Raine in tow, I would appear to be older to people. That might be a good thing, I realized.

"I understand, robot. Carry on with your duties."

I went around the different departments of the store and picked up what I could. Three cans of beef stew. A carton of milk, one day day short of expiration. The last loaf of bread, squashed in the middle. Three packs of cigarettes for Dave. When I was done, I didn't have much in my cart. My stomach ached with hunger in anticipation of the small meals we'd be having.

I went to the cashier, another robot, who waved her finger at each item and put them in plastic bags.

"I'm afraid, ma'am, that I can only sell you two packs of cigarettes per day."

"Fine." I put the other pack back where I found it.

Dave would not be happy, but I was glad he'd be cutting down a bit. Three packs a day was excessive.

CHAPTER SIX

—— ● ——

DAVE

I decided to go in early on my first day. The key card let me in. The lights immediately came on and I saw that the studio was clean, white, and very modern, like almost everything else on Artania.

The robots took only a moment to wake. There were four of them, and three of them immediately began to work on storyboards. The fourth, who looked a little more man-like than the others, approached me.

"Greetings Mr. Watson. My name is Mark. I am a writer. These other three robots are artists. Let me show you to your office."

Mark led me to a private office, walled off from the rest of the space with glass. I would be in a perfect position to observe the robots work.

My office had a steel topped desk, a rolling chair made of white plastic, and a tri-vi art easel. A steel easel was in one corner, with a set of pens and brushes, in case I had an urge to create art the old-fashioned way on canvas or paper. All seemed in order, though it was far more advanced a studio than any I'd used on my home world. I turned to Mark, and asked. "What's the job? They said you'd explain it."

The robot sat down on the edge of my desk and dangled his feet, in a manner very human-like, and waited until I sat down on my chair.

"Mr. Watson —"

"Call me Dave."

"Dave, the book you illustrated five years ago, *The Lonely Scout*, was a best seller throughout Known Space. I realize that since you were an employee of the publisher, not an independent artist, you got only a tiny royalty for your work."

"How do you know that?" I was alarmed they knew so much about me, including my private business dealings.

"Dave, you will find out quite quickly that there are few secrets you can keep from the Artanian government."

"OK, what's your point?"

"We have purchased the rights from the author to write a series of books based on the 'Lonely Scout' character. You are being asked to illustrate six more titles to continue the series."

"That doesn't make sense. The Lonely Scout died at the end of the book."

"He did not die, he got sucked into a wormhole and the wormhole collapsed. We can easily say he got safely to the other side and had more adventures."

———————

A robot came in with a cup of coffee and a pack of cigarettes, my favorite brand. I drank the coffee, realized it had just the right amount of cream and sugar, and lit up. I was not used to being pampered this way, and realized I might grow to like it. Then, it occurred to me to wonder how they knew exactly how much cream and sugar I put in my coffee. And how had they known my brand of cigarettes?

"The whole point of the book was that the Lonely Scout makes the ultimate sacrifice for humanity," I said to Mark. "If we bring him back to life, the point of the first book is lost." I was speaking to Mark as if he was human, I realized.

"Well, Dave, I think when you read the books, you will find we have very elegantly solved that problem. At the end of the seventh book, he will make a sacrifice much bigger than losing his life."

"The books are already written?"

"Yes, I wrote them yesterday."

"All six, in one day?"

"Well, uh, they are children's books, only a few thousand words each."

I had a deep suspicion he was withholding something.

"How long, exactly, did you take to write all six books?"

"Uh — less than an hour."

"Mark, tell me the truth. How long did it take to write all six books?"

"Two point five seven nine seconds."

The answer floored me. It had taken Roger Bellam, the human author of *The Lonely Scout* five years to complete his book. The effort had been agonizing to him, and he had almost overdosed on *zzizzit* in the process. But such was the birth pains of great art. The robot's books had been spun out effortlessly by a machine. They had to be trash.

"Let me see these books."

The tri-vi easel responded to my voice and I saw the first page of the first book.

"The Lonely Scout," I read, "his engines frozen over from a century trapped in the wormhole, woke up to see, he had entered a new star system. And through his bridge view ports, he could see, a brand new world, green and blue and fluffy white. And on this world's surface, his scanners could read, unidentified life signs, plant and animal. And he knew that he had found, a new home for the human race, and he rejoiced in knowing it."

"Well?" Mark asked.

"Kind of hokey," I said. But —

"But similar to the writing style of the first book, right?"

It was. But I had to argue.

"Is this really the best you can do?"

Mark hesitated.

"I asked, is this the best you can do?"

"The point," said Mark, "is not to write the best book that can be written, but to write a book that is so similar in style to the first book, so that children will believe it was written by the same author."

"But it will be well known that Roger didn't write this book."

"Mr. Bellam will get credit for writing all six of the new books, and get a generous royalty. That's in the contract."

I had a bad thought.

"But — if you can write a book that people will believe was written by Roger, you can illustrate a book that people will believe was illustrated by me."

Mark hesitated.

"Well?"

Mark continued to hesitate.

"You don't need me, do you?" I asked.

"Yes, we do, Dave," said the robot. "We need you. Let me explain."

I entered the apartment, threw the keys to the ground car in a bowl set up for the purpose, went to the tri-vi and turned it on. I sat down in the easy chair to watch the latest episode of *Captain Thorn, Space Patrol*. The *H.M.S. Broadsword* was approaching an asteroid mine on a clone liberation mission. Everyone was tense, realizing the colonists would put up a fierce resistance to protect what they considered their lawfully owned property. But the Queen had decreed that clones were legal persons, with rights. She would no longer tolerate clones worked to death as slaves, anywhere in Known Space.

Lieutenant Commander John McCann was having a heart-to-heart with the beautiful Ensign Lucielle Jones, assuring her he had full confidence that in the battle to come, she would carry out her duty with bravery and honor. Then — she reached for him, pulled him close, and they started to kiss. The kiss — turned to something more — and Georgia was in the picture, waving her arms.

"Hello!" she shouted at me. "I've been trying to talk to you, Dave."

I picked up the remote and turned off the tri-vi.

"What, Georgia?" I shouted. "*What?*"

"How was your first day at work?"

I stood up and went to the refrigerator, pulled out a beer and opened it. She followed me. "This is the part where you answer my question."

I went back to the living room and sat down again in the easy chair. I did not want to talk about it, so I said nothing. I could tell by the deep frown on her face that I was in trouble. I tried to jump out of the chair and run to the bedroom, but she leaped on top of me. She grabbed my wrists and tried to hold me down. I don't know what had come over her, but she was trying to hurt me, I think.

"What about the girl?" I asked. "She shouldn't see this."

"Raine is at a neighbor girl's apartment playing tri-vi games," she said. "She won't be back for at least an hour."

"You planned to attack me."

"It is long past time, Dave, that we have a fight."

———

"Why do you want to have a fight?"

"Because we've haven't fought so long. I feel that I'm losing you Dave. You're getting farther and farther away from me. Is that true, Dave? Am I losing you?"

"Just because I don't want to talk doesn't mean you're losing me. It just means, I don't want to talk."

She was trying to bite me now. It was all I could to do to hold her face with one hand while holding her wrists with my other hand. We fell to the floor, and I landed on top of her.

"Please, Georgia. Stop trying to hurt me."

"Will you talk?"

"There's nothing to talk about."

She tried to knee me in the groin, but missed when I rolled. But now, she was on top of me.

"OK, we'll talk," I said. She relaxed, but I was still holding her wrists and face.

"You can let go, Dave. I'll stop."

I wasn't sure I could trust her, but I let go. She got off of me, and went to sit down on the sofa. I stood up and sat in the easy chair. I grabbed my beer and took a long chug.

"God," I muttered, "what the hell am I supposed to do with this woman?"

"Are you talking to God again?"

"What do you want to talk about?" I asked.

"I asked you how your first day at work went. You went to get a beer. So I know, it's bad. I'm your wife, Dave, it's my job to listen to your problems. Let me do my job."

I sat back and tried to focus.

"What if I told you, that humans don't matter anymore. That *I* don't matter anymore."

"Well, Dave, that's a very pessimistic thing to say. I'd ask you to back it up."

"They want to publish six more *Lonely Scout* books, and they want me to illustrate them."

"That's very good news, Dave. What's the problem?"

"They don't need me to do the job," I said. "They just want me to pretend I'm doing it."

Georgia frowned. I could tell she was thinking.

"Let me guess, they have robots who have already illustrated the books."

She was smart, that's one thing you could say about her.

"Correct."

"And the illustrations look exactly like you did them."

"Correct."

"And they've offered you generous royalties to pretend you did them."

"Correct."

"And now, you don't know what to do. Whether to take the money, smile, and live a lie, or expose the fraud and take the consequences."

"Correct."

Georgia stood up and started pacing the room.

"I don't know, Dave. That's a real tough problem. Do you want my advice, or do you want to figure this out yourself?"

I thought it over.

"There must be other options."

"Like what?"

"I could refuse to cooperate, but promise I won't expose them."

"You could do that, but without your cooperation, they would never dare to publish the books, for fear you *might* expose them later. Their plans would be thwarted, so it's the same. They would be angry."

"I could tell them that I insist on doing all the illustrations myself."

"How long would it take you?"

"I don't know, there's at least fifty or sixty illustrations. A year, a year and a half?"

"If you rushed."

"Right."

"No doubt, that would anger them also. They want the books published now, not a year or two from now."

"So, what are you driving at?"

"There's only two possible options," Georgia said, "with only two possible results. They get what they want, or they don't."

I thought about it.

"Ultimately, it's my decision," I said. "But this affects both of us."

"And Raine."

"What?"

"This effects Raine, Dave. She's our foster-daughter. If you rat out these people and embarrass them, the horrible things they do to get revenge on us will also happen to her."

"Oh, God," I said. "I didn't think of that."

"You should think about it, Dave," said Georgia, "Raine's an innocent five-year-old and has already suffered enough. If you choose not to cooperate, she will suffer as we suffer. If you choose to cooperate, she will prosper as we prosper."

"What the hell do I do?"

Georgia looked at me. "What is God telling you to do?"

"Don't do it. Don't be part of a fraud."

"What is your heart telling you?"

"I can't listen to God, not this time."

She came over to me, sat in my lap, put her arms around me.

"You're doing the right thing, Dave," she whispered. "It feels wrong, but it's the right thing."

CHAPTER SEVEN

◯

GEORGIA

The doorbell rang at ten, right on time. A woman in swanky clothes was there, I showed her in. Her name was Lady Annabelle McMartin. She was one of the top personal secretaries on Artania. She had a reputation of taking nobodies and helping them rocket to the top of Artanian society. We were her project now, me and Dave.

She swept by me, smelling of lilac. Following her was her secretary, the secretary to the secretary. His name was Sir Richard Richards. He was wearing cologne that smelled like a broken-in leather saddle, reminding me of my days as a girl when I lived on my grandfather's ranch. It was a masculine smell, and he looked to be very manly. But I knew he was a poof when he glanced at me and sniffed disdainfully.

A young girl came in after them, Miss Josephine Crane. I was told she was to be my new nanny. She told me she was a student at Artania U., studying to be xeno-biologist. Her specialty was the Hinni, the native species of this world. I was about to object that I didn't need a nanny, when a fourth person walked in, announced she was my new interior decorator, and immediately started criticizing my taste in furniture, wallpaper, and decor. She handed me a card identifying her as Madame Rochelle, no last name. Later I looked her up on the Weave and learned she was in the top five in her profession. I never got the chance to tell her that none of the style choices in the apartment had been mine.

My data-com rang, it was Dave: "They told me a personal secretary was coming," I told him, "but they sent an army."

"OK," said Dave. "Promise me you won't freak out, but you have a private audience with the Queen at tea time this afternoon."

"What? I have nothing to wear."

"They're sending people to make sure you look presentable - a wardrobe person, hairdresser, beautician — "

"I get that you're publishing a series of children's books, Dave, but what's going on? Illustrators don't usually get this kind of roll-out-the-carpet treatment."

"These aren't just children's books, Georgia. The government of Artania is fighting a war of ideas against the wrong-headed ideology of retreat and retrenchment put forward by the Home Party. Nothing less than the fate of humanity is at stake. We will either be a space-faring race of explorers and conquerers, or we will be stuck forever on one dying world. Since I am the illustrator of these books, I am a very important person right now. They have asked me to go on a tour of all the major cities around Artania to be a spokesman for the notion that its the human race's destiny to reach for the stars and all the worlds around them."

I hesitated.

"I'm glad to see you've finally taking an interest in what's happening, Dave," I said. "Just don't let this get to your head."

Why did I say that? I regretted it immediately. He responded, his voice full of ice: "Of course not, dear. I would never let it get to my head. I will always have you around to remind me that none of this is actually earned."

"I didn't mean —"

I heard a click as he hung up.

They sent an air limo to pick me up. I arrived at the Queen's Palace at three thirty and was quickly shown to the parlor. It was exactly four when the steward guiding me knocked on the door, and we were allowed entry. He ushered me in, and closed the door.

A woman in white greeted me. Her red hair was even redder than mine. "Come in, Mrs. Watson, no, don't try to curtsy to me, I know you've just arrived on our world and won't stand on ceremony. Also, I know they told you to address me as 'your majesty' but during this meeting let's be on a first name basis. You can call me 'Artania' and I will call you 'Georgia'. Agreed?"

She was the Queen, so what choice did I have other than to agree with her? I said, "Agreed."

She invited me to sit and then poured the tea for us. She put two lumps of sugar in mine, and a bit of cream, exactly how I liked it. Then, she handed me my cup.

I knew what she was doing. She was impressing on me the fact that she knew every detail about me, which meant we were being watched.

She smiled, I smiled, measuring each other for strengths and weaknesses. At last, she spoke:

"I understand you and your husband may have had an unpleasant journey to our world, and an uncomfortable stay at one of our camps. If that is the case, I apologize on behalf of my government."

"There is no need for apology, your majesty — Artania. You saved us from a Home Party death camp and provided us with a beautiful new home here on your world. We will be eternally grateful for your generosity."

"I'm glad to hear you say that, Georgia, I really am. It helps me get to the point of why I've asked you to have tea with me today."

Here it comes. She had shown me the velvet glove of gentility and politeness. Now she would take it off and reveal the iron fist beneath it.

"I have heard that you and your husband have concerns that the way we are creating this work of children's literature *The Lonely Scout* book series might be unethical in some way. Isn't that so?"

There was no point denying it. Her spies had no doubt recorded every conversation we'd had on the topic.

"We did have concerns," I said. "But we have refined our views over time."

"I see." She knew I was lying. Just this morning I had told Dave not to let all his new fame get to his head, because, as he put it, his new fame was unearned. "Let me explain to you, my view, the Artanian view, about this new technology we are using to help Dave create these illustrations. Let us imagine, a cave dwelling Neanderthal living one hundred thousand years ago. He is a hunter, and he uses his finger to create cave paintings, to make a record of his kills of dangerous beasts and the glory they've earned for him in his tribe."

The Queen paused. I realized she wanted me to respond. "I can imagine that."

"Now, let us imagine that some other fellow in the tribe has glued together pieces of hair and a piece of wood and somehow invented the paintbrush. He presents it to his friend, the hunter, and says: "Use this, it will improve the quality of your cave paintings." And what do you guess the hunter says in return?"

So this was to be a guessing game. I would play. "The hunter says, this brush, unlike my finger, is not a part of me. If I use it, it won't really be my painting."

The Queen's eyes narrowed. "You are a lot more intelligent than I expected, Georgia. Why is a woman as clever as you content to be a housewife?"

A compliment, combined skillfully with a calculated insult.

"You are content to be Queen of a Constitutional Monarchy. Certainly a woman of your intelligence grows weary of waving at parades and smashing champagne bottles on newly constructed starships."

Her face flushed with anger. I'd heard she had a temper, but wow.

"Don't make the mistake of underestimating me, Georgia. I have real power beneath these layers of pomp and ceremony I use to disguise myself."

I had irked her. I had won this round. I waited until she'd calmed down a bit.

"You were talking about the painter who refuses to use a paintbrush."

"Right, well you see my point, I don't have to spell it out, do I?"

"You are saying, that when a robot creates a work of art, imitating the style of a human artist, it is as if the artist had created it himself."

"Right, because a robot's work imitating a human artist is indistinguishable from the work of that human artist. Also, the robot is not actually creating, it is mechanically imitating the style of a human creator. The robot is like a paintbrush in the hand of the artist, an extension of the artist that does not change the fact that it is the artist's work."

"Not everyone is going to buy that bill of goods. I don't."

Artania's eyes widened in surprise, and again her face turned red. But only for a moment.

"You are right, not everyone would buy it, which is why secrecy is so important. The public must believe that the human writer and the human illustrator created these new books without the assistance of robots."

"I understand. I can keep a secret."

"But you don't understand, and that's why you're here."

———————

"Why am I here?"

"Georgia, let me explain it. You may never believe that your husband illustrated these books. You may never 'buy the bill of goods.' That is acceptable to me, I don't care what you believe. But it is important, critical even, that your husband 'buy the bill of goods.' He must believe, in his heart, that the illustrations in the books are truly his work."

"Why?"

"Because while he is on tour, he will be scrutinized, prodded, probed, by critics and members of the book reading public. If he believes himself to be a fraud, these people will realize it, and he will be exposed as a fraud."

"How can he ever believe he created the work? It was created by the robots before he arrived at the studio that first Monday morning."

"He will come to believe because it is in his best interests to believe. He will believe it as firmly as he believes in God."

"How does that come into it?"

"Your husband is a man of unusually strong faith. He told me, last week when I met him for tea, that the reason he first approached you was because God told him to."

"He's told me that too. What of it?"

"A man like Dave is rare. His faith in God is so strong, he hears God's voice giving him advice and counsel. Dave consults with God in all his major decisions."

"God told him not to be part of this scheme. I'm sure you know that."

"I do. That is why it's so critical you listen to me, Georgia. You must be the voice that opposes God."

"I did that when I talked him into this scheme."

"Yes, you did do that, but just this morning you told Dave not to let his new fame get to his head. By saying that, you were telling him you didn't believe he was the true artist. Why did you do that?"

I was taken aback. Why did I do that?

"I'm a truthful person. I wanted him to realize he's not the real artist."

"What possible good reason would you have to remind him of that?"

"I don't — I don't know."

"Right, you don't know. I will tell you the reason. You tell the truth, because it's the truth. You are a woman who grew up on a horse ranch in a backwards agricultural world and in that simple world you lived in people tell the truth because it's the truth. I honor that. I respect it. I would give almost anything to live in a world like that, where people tell the truth because it's the truth. But you, Georgia, are now living in *my* world, the high stakes world of war, espionage and politics where death is lurking around every corner. If you're not careful, your simple truthful ways will lead to the destruction of you, your husband, and your daughter Raine."

I realized I was trembling.

"Are you — threatening me?"

"No, absolutely not. I am simply telling you the way it is. Think about what we're trying to do, and the enemies arrayed against us. These children's books are part of a much larger propaganda campaign aimed at winning the war. The Artanian government and entertainment industry have combined their efforts to create tri-vi movies, tri-vi shows, books, comic books, games, you name it, to convince the human race that it is not our fate to crawl down a hole and die. *The Lonely Scout* is extremely important in this effort, since it eloquently makes the argument that we humans should be exploring space and conquering new worlds in a way that children can understand. Do you know what the Home Party has done to Earth's scouting service? They have completely disbanded it, sold off the scout ships for scrap. They have stopped cold the exploration of new worlds for humanity to inhabit. Do you realize what that means for humanity? If the human race doesn't expand, Georgia, we die. History has proven that, over and over. The Home Party is trying to kill us — the entire human race — by restricting us to one world. If we don't fight these fanatics with everything we have, they will succeed."

She paused, out of breath.

"But the Hinni," I said, "we've done terrible things to them. We rounded them up, forced them to live on reservations. We've made the Aurox into slaves. The species that inhabited Sheng was exterminated."

"Yes! We humans are ruthless to the other sentient species we encounter. The Home Party has very good arguments, convincing to billions of people. They may even have the moral high ground, if such a thing exists. But if we accept what they say, and retreat to Earth, we humans will lose all hope for the future and die."

"Why are you putting all this on me? I'm just one person."

"You are the wife of one of our top creators. You have the power to boost your husband's confidence in himself, but instead, you are tearing him down. All because you believe that telling the truth is so important, nothing else matters. Do you understand what folly that is? The survival of all us is on the line, and you want to risk it all because you can't stand your husband being involved in something you consider unethical. I am asking you, Georgia, I am begging you, please put aside your provincial code of morality and think about the bigger picture. Are you listening to me? Please tell me that you understand what I am saying."

I didn't know what to say. The Queen had overwhelmed me with her words. I needed time to think.

"Well?" she pressed.

"I will consider what you've said very seriously. Let me go back to my husband and talk it over with him."

"What? Damn it, Georgia. I must have your answer now. I won't let you leave the palace until I have your answer."

I put the tea cup down and stood up.

"It has been a pleasure meeting you, your majesty. The experience has been — enlightening."

"Don't you try to leave, Georgia. I swear —"

I walked to the door and opened it. Nothing happened.

I closed the door behind me. Again, nothing.

I walked down the hall, turned, and walked down another hall, every moment an agony.

I got into the elevator and pushed the button to the lowest floor.

Finally, I left the palace through the giant front doors and found the air limo on the landing platform, its robot driver waiting for me.

"Home," I said. As the limo took off, I finally relaxed.

I had called the Queen's bluff. Every moment, I'd expected her to do send someone to stop me, drag me back to her.

But she had let me go.

She still held all the most powerful cards.

I would have to think carefully before making my next move. I would talk to Dave first.

CHAPTER EIGHT

DAVE

It was around six in the evening, and the sky was darkening in the east. I was in the studio with my robots when Georgia barged in, uninvited.

"We need to talk," she demanded, "tell your helpers to take a break."

"We have a lot of work to do," I said. "Can it wait?"

"No, it can't wait," she said. "We have important decisions to make about the viability of this entire project."

"Georgia, really, it's not your project, it's mine, and you have no say whatsoever. Go home and make dinner. I'll be home by nine."

Georgia raised her fist to hit me, but Mark said: "We'll leave, Dave, so you and Mrs. Watson can talk."

"No, Mark," I said, "send out the other robots, but you stay. I trust your counsel, and I want you to be here if any major decisions are to be made."

The other robots left the studio, leaving me, my wife, and Mark.

"*What?*" I asked, a bit impatiently.

"Don't speak to me in that tone."

"You march in here, demand I drop everything I'm doing, so we can have another discussion. So go on, tell me what you want to tell me, so I can go back to work."

"The Queen and I had tea today," I said.

"I know that, Georgia. I'm the one who told you she wanted to have tea with you."

"She threatened us, Dave. She said if we didn't cooperate with this scheme of hers, our whole family would be destroyed."

There was a long pause as I took that in.

"The Queen is known to have a mercurial temper, Mrs. Watson," said Mark at last. "She often says things she doesn't mean. Pay it no mind."

"Gearbox, if I want your input, I'll ask for it."

"So, she threatened you," I said. "What did you expect? You talked me into doing this, but ever since, you've had regrets. No doubt, she wanted to set you straight. I can't really blame her if she got a bit over-dramatic to convince you of the importance of what we're doing."

Her reaction was a look of horror, and I knew I'd said the wrong thing. "She threatened *Raine*. If it was just you or me she threatened, I could forgive her. But she threatened the life of a five-year-old child. She's a *monster*."

"Like I said, Mrs. Watson," Mark said, "the Queen frequently loses her temper and says things she later regrets. I would not be surprised if she called you tomorrow morning and begged you to forgive her for what she said. She is really a good woman at heart, not someone you should be afraid of."

"This thing is going to have to leave, Dave," Georgia fumed. "I am your wife and I am entitled to speak with you without a chatterbox machine constantly interrupting me."

I realized I would have to give in to her, again. I nodded at the robot, and he turned to leave.

"Stay close, Mark. We have some important formatting changes to make. I want to put Book Three to bed tonight."

"Yes, Dave." The robot left.

I turned back to see my wife was having a serious crying jag. I wanted to reach out and comfort her, but something held me back.

"What happened to us, Dave? We were so much in love on the day we married, but now, it's all I can do to keep myself from tearing your head off."

"You said you wanted to fight, that we never fought, and that was hurting our marriage. Now, we fight constantly and you're not happy with that either."

"Dave, please, listen to me."

I leaned back against the desk. "I'm listening." But my heart was hardening to her. I didn't want to listen, not really.

"We started down this road because we were afraid. We thought the government would do terrible things to us if we didn't do what they wanted. But Dave, fear is never a good reason to do anything. We gave into fear, and now we're doing things we know are wrong. The guilt, at least my guilt, is destroying our marriage, and when the fraud is revealed, it will destroy your reputation as an artist. There will be no coming back for you, a charge of fraud is a black mark that follows an artist wherever he goes. You won't be able to get work, anywhere. Please Mark, I ask you, let's tell the Queen we've changed our mind. Please, let's turn back while we still can."

She came to me, wanted me to give her a hug, but I roughly pushed her away. She stumbled back, nearly fell down. I don't know why I did that, I'll never be able to explain it. She stiffened at my rejection, and I think that was the moment she decided that she no longer loved me. The look she gave me, I will never forget. It was like she saw me for who I really was, for the first time.

I said, "There is no fraud, Georgia. I've been working on the project for three weeks, and in that time I've made substantial changes. I've completely redone the formatting. I've rearranged the order of some of the illustrations. I've had the robots change some style elements to be more consistent with —"

She started to laugh. It wasn't a happy laugh, it was more like the laugh of a crazy woman. I didn't like it.

"Listen to yourself, dear husband, you've rearranged a few details and claim the work is really yours after all. I realize now what's going on. Your illustrations in the original *The Lonely Scout* gave you a small claim to fame. Roger's story was brilliant, but the illustrations you provided didn't add or detract to the success of the book. You were lucky, that's all, and you've been offered this opportunity because, again, you've been lucky."

"No, Georgia. This is God's plan. He tells me every day that —"

"God doesn't tell you anything, you stupid jackass. When you hear voices in your head, it means you're insane. I was a fool to ever get involved with you. When you told me that first time that God talked to you, I should have run away and never looked back. But instead, I married you after knowing you a mere three weeks. I was a stupid girl, and I've paid for it with two miserable years trying to get you to act like a decent person to me. But you can't, can you? You can't show me love, because you don't even love yourself. I'm going home to pack up my things and Raine's things. We will move to another world, so our paths never cross yours again."

She had finally seen through me. I knew, even in the beginning, she eventually would, and on that day, she would leave. But I wouldn't let her go, even though I knew it would be the best thing for both of us. I said, my voice full of cruelty, "You're not thinking, Georgia. What about Raine? If you break up our marriage, you will dash all her hopes of ever having a stable family. Can you do that, to a poor miserable orphan? Can you break her heart? You have to stay, for her sake."

Her eyes widened, and I knew that now, she really hated me. "Damn you, Dave. Damn you to hell. How dare you use emotional blackmail to keep me trapped in this unhappy marriage. How can you live with yourself, knowing that — "

I interrupted her rant. "I'm right, Georgia, and you know it. You love Raine, and you can't hurt her with the trauma of her new parents divorcing. You will stay with me, because you must."

She rushed at me, beat my chest furiously, tripped me, and knocked me to the ground. She kicked me without mercy as I lay there. She kicked my face, my chest, my stomach, my arms, my legs. She broke a rib or two. I lost a tooth. I did nothing to defend myself, I didn't even go into fetal position. I knew I would have to endure this, but afterwards she would stay.

At long last, she sat down cross-legged on the floor besides me. Exhausted. Defeated.

I sat up, held my ribs, and winced with the pain. I said:

"This is what's going to happen."

She said nothing, but I knew she was listening.

"I will complete the work on the project, and we will get all six books published early next month. After publication, I will spend a year touring the major cities of Artania, speaking about the books, and telling the universe that humanity must not give up on space travel and exploration. You and Raine will accompany me on the tour. You will be a dutiful wife, and you will make sure Raine is a dutiful child. For appearances sake, we will act like a happy, loving family. We will make lots of money, and we will split it fifty-fifty. When the year is over, if you still want to leave me, we will get a divorce. You may keep Raine all to yourself, I have no interest in being her father after you're gone. You will never breathe a word to anyone that you think the work is not really mine. If you do, I will sue you for defamation. I will win and take you for everything you have, including Raine. Do we have an understanding?"

She muttered.

"Do we have an understanding?"

"Yes."

"I will go to the emergency room now and have my wounds looked after. I will not report you to the police for domestic abuse, you're welcome. You will go home and make dinner. I will be home at nine, and I expect it to be hot. We will eat dinner as a family. Do we have an understanding?"

She muttered again.

"What was that?"

"Yes. But you won't get away with it. Someone will figure out you didn't really create these illustrations. Then — "

"We will deal with that situation if it happens. Understood?"

"Yes."

She was defeated for now, but I knew it wouldn't be long before she was plotting some sort of revenge. From now on, I would have to watch my back.

CHAPTER NINE

GEORGIA

Most books in a book series are published one year apart, to maximize interest in each book with the reading public, and to maximize profits. But the Queen was in a hurry, so all six books of *The Lonely Scout* series were published on one day. The first book was re-released, and all seven were sold in a boxed set. The publish date was chosen for maximum propaganda impact: Seven-Seven-Ten, the third anniversary of the terrorist attacks that allowed the Home Party to seize power on Earth, and started Earth's war with her colonies. The release date made it clear that the book series was intended as a propaganda counter-attack on the Home Party and everything it stood for. The pre-release buzz, whipped up by the Weave sheets and tri-vi channels, guaranteed blockbuster sales. Lines of children, and their parents, waited to buy the books at bookstores in every world in Known Space not under Coalition control. All seven of the books instantly shot to the top of the *Hun Wat Herald* best seller's list, and stayed there, week after week. Everyone was talking about the lonely little scout ship who got lonelier and more homesick the further he traveled from

Earth, but realized in the end, that Home was any world you landed on. It was mankind's destiny that one day, the whole galaxy would be Home.

The Queen read the books to children who visited the Palace. Mothers and fathers read it to their own children. Grown-ups, realizing the books were not just for children, bought the set to read themselves. And no one's eyes were dry when the Lonely Scout threw himself into the core of an exploding neutron star, to save the human race he loved so much from ultimate destruction.

The books were hated by members of the Home Party as much as it was loved by everyone else. They denounced it as humanocentric and imperialistic, glorifying the human race for all its worst faults. There were bomb threats against the man given credit as the author, Roger Bellac, who had to be moved from a nursing home to a more secure location. A bomb actually did go off in a bookstore in Spiro, killing three humans and seven Aurox. But these threats were muted compared to the overwhelming love children and adults alike showed towards the books and the character Lonely Scout. There were Lonely Scout toys, games, bedsheets, cereal boxes, the possibilities were limited only by human creativity and human greed. The books got rave reviews, and won all five major science fiction awards. The love and attention was heady for Dave Watson, who as illustrator, shared the glory with the author. But the author was sick and unavailable, so in his place the real love was aimed at the robot Mark, who as author's assistant had a deep knowledge of the story and it's meaning.

The tour started on the release date in North City, then progressed through West City, East City, and South City, with the grand finish in Central City. On the one year anniversary of the release date, the Queen planned an event that would commemorate the fourth anniversary of Seven-Seven-Seven and allow my husband, illustrator Dave Watson and robot author-stand-in Mark, to have one last hurrah before adoring fans and critics, before going back to their normal hum-drum lives.

———————

We were in our hotel room, getting prepared for the final party that would end our tour.

"Where the hell is my tie?" Dave wanted to know. As the tour progressed, Dave had been drinking more and more. It was a rare event, like a solar eclipse, to see him sober.

"It's around your neck, jackass," I snarled, rolling my eyes. This was the final night I would have to play dutiful wife to the great illustrator. In the morning, I would serve divorce papers and start my new life. With half of the royalties Dave had taken in, I could buy a mansion. I had a nice property picked out on High Mesa, and had instructed my agent to make an offer that was ten million Artanian dollars below the asking price. I was certain the offer would be snapped up quickly, given the depressed war-time market.

"Oh, there it is," Dave found the tie with shaking fingers.

"Let me help you, Daddy," said Raine, now six-years-old. She stood on a chair and tied her foster-father's tie with a well practiced hand. Dave and Raine, despite Dave's initial reluctance to be a father, had developed a deep bond during the year of the tour. The orphan girl was Dave's constant companion, and their favorite activity was reading the books together. She loved the story, and could recite much of it by heart. She adored the colorful illustrations, and bragged to everyone she met that her Daddy and drawn them. Everyone on the tour loved her, and for the first time she was surrounded by so much affection that she almost forgot the trauma of her past. But still she had nightmares, and would wake up screaming. Dave would quickly run to her bedside, and hold her in his arms until she fell asleep again.

The whole thing was a horror show, I realized, because tomorrow I would have to break both their hearts and announce that I was going through with the divorce. Things between me and Dave had not improved. I pretended love and affection in front of fans, but behind closed doors I was cold to him. I avoided starting open battle with Mark, so as to avoid upsetting Raine. But silently, we waged a bitter cold war against each other of petty insults and bitter recriminations.

Lately, though, he had attempted to make amends. He was motivated, I was certain, by the realization that when I left him, I would take Raine with me. "Please, darling," he would say. "We loved each other once. Isn't it possible there is still a spark left of the love we had that could be rekindled?" But I would have none of it. His two years of neglect and refusal to face our problems had hardened my heart to him. The final outrage, when he shoved me away violently as I tried to embrace him, ate away at my heart, soured my soul. I would not be happy until I was well away from him, and didn't have his presence as a reminder of every time I'd tried to show him love and he had responded with indifference.

But tonight in our dressing room, even though he was drunk, or maybe because of it, he looked at me with longing bordering on despair at the love we had lost. I knew what he was trying to do, he had done it before, and before I had tried to ignore him. But this time, I was enraged, and I turned around to confront him. Raine was in the room, but I lost my mind.

"You have no right to look at me like that, Dave. No right." Tears formed in my eyes.

"You were the woman who wore a green dress and picked a white flower. Do you remember?"

"Oh my God, stop it!" I lost all control as tears ran down my face.

"Mommy," said Raine, starting to cry. "Please don't shout at Daddy."

"God told me you'd be mine if only I worked up the courage to talk to you."

I put my hands over my ears to try to keep out the sound of his voice.

"I took you to coffee, and we fell in love."

"It's too late, Dave. You had your chance, but it's too late." I was a complete wreck now. Raine was falling apart too. I realized I was doing a terrible thing, hurting her like this.

Dave fell to his knees, held out the wedding ring I had thrown at him last week.

"Please, Georgia. I'm a different man now. Can't you see it? I don't want to lose you. I don't want to lose Raine. Please, take me back and I will spend the rest of my life trying to make amends for the years I was cruel to you."

———————

I turned my back to him.

"You're no longer the bastard you were, but now you're a drunkard."

"I will swear off all alcohol if you take me back."

"I would be a fool to forgive you."

"Let us both be fools. Let us love each other and be fools."

I turned around to face him again. He was lost, broken, hopeless. I could heal his brokenness with my love, but I wanted nothing to do with him.

But then I noticed Raine. She was clinging to her father, her face buried in his chest, seeking solace for her misery - the misery I had caused her. I knew then, that if I left Dave, Raine would choose him over me. I could fight it in court, but there was no preference for mother over father in modern divorce law, such a preference was a relic of a long ago past. I realized that I had lost my daughter, and the only way to get her back was to return to my husband, and find someway to find peace with him.

There might be a way.

"Sing it to me, Dave, sing the song you wrote the day we met. Sing it to help me remember what we had."

"I don't know if I can remember the words."

"You must remember the words, Dave. This won't work if you can't remember the words."

Still on his knees, Dave closed his eyes, leaned back his head, and sang:

*In the grassy field, the woman in green picked a
white flower.
In that moment, I fell in love with her.
I prayed to God, "Let her be mine."
God said to me: "If you want her, go talk to her."
I said: "I will."
I walked up to the woman in green.
She turned, her red hair flowing, and said to me,
"Oh, a man. How do you do?"
"I was fine," I said, "until I saw you. Now, my heart is
filled with wanting something I can't have."
"What is it?" she asked. "That you can't have?"*

"You."

She smiled. "Who ever told you, I was something you can't have."

I smiled back. "Would you like some coffee?"

"I would love some coffee," she said.

That was the beginning.

"It's not a good song, Dave. Too many notes in some places, not enough in others. The words are uninspired. Had I not been there, and experienced these events myself, I would never consider this song to be worthy of anything but indifference, nay contempt, at the clumsiness which with it is constructed."

"But it makes you remember the love we once had, and now have lost?" Dave asked.

"It doesn't make me remember my love for you, but it makes me remember that once there was a woman, who met a man, and was intrigued by him."

"You were intrigued because of your sexual attraction to this man?"

"No, that's not it. I was intrigued that a man, so handsome and charming, believed that I, a somewhat overweight woman, was something he could not ever have. He either had a very low opinion of himself, or such an exalted opinion of me that I was practically a goddess in his mind. I had to know which, so when he invited me to have coffee, I said 'yes.'"

"Does hearing this song make you want to renew your friendship with this man? If you can't remember our love, perhaps you can remember we were friends?"

"Friendship between a man and a woman is such a will-o-wisp, isn't it? In most cases, either the man or the woman is engaged in deceit, wanting more than friendship, but saying otherwise to avoid losing the friend. It almost always leads to a bad end, when one reveals his or her true feelings to the other, and is rejected."

"So, you don't remember our love and believe we can't be friends, what can we be to each other?"

I thought about it.

"Co-parents."

"Of course, we will always be that."

"Companions."

"How do you define 'companion'?"

"A companion is one who is in your company, more often than not. You share meals with a companion. You might share a bed. A companion can be relied upon to aid you when you face an enemy, and you will aid her when she faces his. A companion will not abandon you when times are tough, and you will not abandon her. A companion is more than a friend, but less. Friends come and go, but a companion is always there. A friend has affection for you, and will stop being a friend when that affection ends. A companion need have no affection for you, she may even dislike you intensely, but that doesn't matter. She remains a companion, and you remain hers. It is a bond that can't be broken by loss of affection. A companion is there for you because it is in her best interest to be there for you. It is a bond of mutual self-interest. Each companion lives in a less dangerous world because she has a companion."

"Do you believe, Georgia, that we can be companions?"

"I believe we can. I will never again love you, or even remember loving you. I have no affection for you. But we can be companions."

"Will you wear the ring, as a symbol of our companionship?"

"I will, because we remain husband and wife, and that's a relationship that is stronger when one is also a companion."

"Do you wish to resume our sexual relations?"

I realized this was a critical question. Dave was a man, and if I denied him my bed, he would seek companionship with other women. This would run the risk that he would fall in love with one of these women, and once again, I'd face the possibility of divorce and losing Raine.

"We will share the wedding bed," I said. "But as companions, not as lovers."

Dave grinned with joy, and stood up. As he took my hand and put the wedding ring back on my finger, I wondered why he was willing to accept so little from me. I had to assume he hoped that with us sharing companionship and our bodies, more would develop between us. I looked at Raine, and saw that she was smiling. She might not understand everything that had transpired, but she knew there would now be peace where before there had been rancor.

I could never admit the truth to either of them, for in telling it, I might lose them both. Everything I had said to Dave was a lie. I did not wish to be his companion. I detested the thought of being his bedmate. But I had chosen to be both because my dreams for a future life of happiness without Dave were dashed when I realized I'd lose Raine if I tried to make those dreams a reality.

COLONY

CHAPTER ONE

AMY

I was talking to the young man in the brown uniform. They had sent me here to talk to him. I had worn the green overalls of a farmer. He would expect a girl like me, a colonist, to be dressed like that. If I had dressed nice, he might have been suspicious.

"So. You're a scientist," I said. It wasn't a question. It was a statement. He had told me, less than an hour ago, that he was.

"Yes."

"Sent by the Empire." He had told me that too. Why was I making him repeat himself?

"Yes."

"You're only a boy." He was. I'd been watching him a week, from a hidden place in the forest. In that time he hadn't shaved, and barely had a stubble.

"You're only a girl, so we're even." He smiled. That made his cute face even cuter. He had blond hair and blue eyes, just like me. But I had a job to do, and had to focus. I could not — *would not* — start to like him. My job was to *pretend* to like him. If I started to like him, I couldn't do what I had come to do.

"How old are you?" I asked.

"Seventeen," he said. "How old are you?"

"Sixteen," I lied. I was fourteen. But he was an off-worlder, and I knew how he would react if he knew I was fourteen. He'd think of me as a child and would lose interest. Pa and the other men had told me to keep him interested, so I lied and said I was sixteen.

I looked around his camp. He had parked his ship in a flattened area next to a lake. A fuel hose went from the ship to the lake, so there was a water converter aboard. The ship was small, big enough for him and three passengers. But he had come to my world alone.

A mistake.

He had built a tent ten meters from the ship, big enough for a bunk and some of his personal belongings. The tent was brown, like his uniform. He had already given me a tour. He had real books — left over from the days when there was no Weave, no tri-vi, and people read things on paper. He was proud of his books — showed me one called *Moby Dick*. "Call me Ishmael," it had started. I tried to read further, but lost interest and put it down.

He had built a campfire, which was unlit now, during the day, and on the other side of the fire he had planted the Imperial flag. The flag had a dark blue field with three white stars in the center, representing the Alliance worlds that had defeated Earth during the Fifth War, surrounded by a multi-colored circle representing the Unity of humans, Hinni, Aurox, robots and clones. Thirty-eight smaller white stars, representing the minor colony worlds, were outside the circle, arrayed in a random pattern. In the century since the Fifth War had ended, humanity had spread over a much larger area than forty-one systems, but the Empire hadn't changed the flag. I realized, in that moment, that the flag represented the problem the newer colonies had with the Empire.

But I had to keep my mind focused on the pressing problem, which was the Empire's presence on our world, represented by this boy.

"Dr. Carver," I started. "I —"

"Please Miss Branagan, call me John. Can I call you Amy?"

Maybe he was getting interested, since he now wanted to be on a first name basis.

"Of course, John."

"What were you going to say, Amy?"

"Your mission here on my world would be much easier if you had a guide."

"I realize that, Amy. Are you offering your services?"

"I am." Would it really be this easy?

"I have nothing in my budget for a guide," he said. "So I'd have to pay you out of my own pocket. Would ten dollars a day be sufficient?"

I had no idea what "ten dollars" was, and there was nothing I could buy on my world using Imperial money. But I said, so he would not be suspicious: "Twenty dollars."

"Fifteen," he said, still smiling that cute smile of his. I had to avoid looking at his face.

"Sold," I said.

John reached into his pocket, pulled out two coins. He handed them to me, and our fingertips touched, shooting electricity up my arm.

When I was over that shock, I looked at the coins, and was shocked in a different way.

"This is gold."

"Yes."

I had expected that John would give me paper money, which I would have tossed in a drawer as useless. But gold was real. I could actually spend these coins, even here on my remote colony world, fourteen Jumps through wormholes from the borders of the Empire.

John went into his tent, came out again with a backpack, two canteens, and a hand scanner, which was linked to his data-com. He went to the lake and filled up the canteens, then handed one to me. There was a leather strap, and I put it around my shoulder. John put the backpack on his back, and put his canteen around his shoulder. There was a weapon holstered to his belt — probably a laser pistol. I carried a laser pistol myself when I left home and was well-trained in how to use it. It was hidden in a leg holster under my overalls.

"Let's go," he said.

"What would you like to see first?"

"You're the guide," John said. "Lead, and I'll follow."

CHAPTER TWO

─ ⬤ ─

JOHN

Amy led me through the forest two kilometers until we got to the edge of a cave. It was dark inside, so I reached into my backpack, pulled out a flashlight and turned it on. I handed it to the colonist girl, and she walked in. I followed.

We went in fifteen meters and she stopped. "Look up," she said, pointing the flashlight upwards. The beam of light revealed icicle-like solid drippings from the cave ceiling.

"Stalactites," I said. "I've seen the like scores of times." I couldn't help bragging about the worlds I'd explored in my year of being in the Scout Service. Maybe I was trying to impress her.

"Look down," she said, turning the flashlight downwards. Upside-down icicles stuck up from the cave floor.

"Stalagmites," I said. "Again, quite common." Why was I acting like such an ass?

"Can you eat them?" she smiled.

"No," I said, in my best scientist lecture voice, "stalactites and stalagmites are mineral deposits, created by running water. They are inedible."

Amy bent over, pulled at a stalagmite and broke it off the floor. She put it in her mouth and bit off a piece. Then she handed it to me and smiled.

"Try it."

"I'll have to analyze if first. Regulations."

The smile fell off her face. "Don't you trust me?"

I had just met Amy a few hours ago, when she approached my camp while I was analyzing soil samples. I had known there was a human colony on this world, had detected their presence from space, but she had been the first colonist to make contact, one week after I had landed. Did I trust her? Experience, and my training, told me not to. This was an illegal colony, so I should be on my guard.

There was a long, awkward pause.

"John, I don't think I can be your guide if you don't trust me."

I didn't really need a guide, but I wanted her company for other reasons. It had been a year since the last time I'd seen another human, much less a girl my own age. I took a bite of the stalagmite. It tasted like —

"Candy," I said. "It tastes like sugar candy."

"These formations are the secretions of a microscopic organism that lives in the caves," Amy said. "If we ever establish trade relations with the Empire, sugar will be one of our primary exports."

"If?" I asked.

"When," she corrected herself. "I meant 'when', of course 'when'."

She had made a mistake, revealing something she was not supposed to reveal. I was glad I had a laser pistol.

"What's next?"

"You'll like it."

"What?"

"You'll see."

CHAPTER THREE

AMY

I was putting off what I had to do. I decided to show John something beautiful, so he would die having seen it. It was the least I could do. We trekked another five kilometers, and then stopped. I waved my arms dramatically.

"This, John," I said, "is something I'll bet even you haven't seen."

We were on the edge of a mighty chasm, ten kilometers wide, an unknown number of kilometers down. A thick mist covered the top of the chasm, so there was no way to see what lay at the bottom. A mighty river on the opposite side, one kilometer wide, went to the edge of the chasm and fell off as a mighty waterfall that disappeared into the mist. The bottom was so far down, we could not hear the sound of the water landing. Mighty reptilian birds flew through the air, screeching as they hunted for prey. From the surrounding forest, unseen insects and birds contributed to the cacophony. And then there were the Floaters, drifting through the air — glowing brightly with neon pink, green, yellow, orange, purple. Each was two meters wide and trailing a group of tentacles. They emitted a song of such peacefulness and harmony, it made me wish I could stay here forever.

"Down there, John, is an unexplored world," I told the scientist. "We colonists have sent men down to explore it, to see if there's a bottom, but they never return. We have no idea what's down there."

I was lying. John would figure that out soon. And then — I'd have to kill him.

It happened sooner that I thought it would. John picked up his hand scanner and studied it. "The music these floating creatures are making has a pattern to it. I think they're attempting to communicate with us."

I had maneuvered myself so that I was standing behind him. He had not noticed as I had taken my laser pistol out of my leg holster and aimed it at him. It was a small pistol, suited for a woman's hand, but still — quite lethal at close range.

He turned around, and his smile fell away. He knew he was facing death, but he did not seem afraid.

"Well, Amy," he said. "If you're going to shoot me, shoot me. Otherwise, put that thing away so we can talk."

"I'm sorry John, I have orders to kill you," I said. But my resolve was melting. I had killed many animals, sometimes I'd done worse. But I had never killed a human.

"You can kill me after we talk," John said. "Does that seem reasonable?"

I knew he was stalling for time. But I relented.

"Take off your gun belt and throw it to me," I said. "If you do that, we can talk."

John unbuckled his belt and tossed it in my direction. It landed at my feet. I realized he might have other weapons hidden on him, something I hadn't thought of before. At the very least, he would have a knife.

"Throw me your knife."

John pulled up his pant leg, removed a knife, and tossed it to me.

"Now, can we talk?" he asked.

I was a bit put off by his attitude.

"Aren't you upset or angry? I'm about to kill you, John. Doesn't that bother you just a bit?"

"If I thought you were a killer, Amy, I would never have hired you to be my guide."

"You think I'm not a killer? Why not? Because I'm a girl?"

"It's something about the eyes," he said. "Soldiers get a certain look after they've fought in a war too long. My older brother came home from the war for Christmas and I saw it in his eyes. You don't have that look. I know you've never killed a human, or any other sentient being."

He was right, I'd never killed another sentient being. Why had Pa and the other men trusted me with this job?

Because — there was the unspoken assumption that a fourteen-year-old girl would not be perceived as a threat, while a full-grown man would. And they had been right. I had the drop on him.

I couldn't let them down. I resolved to kill this boy as soon as he had said what he wanted to say. It might be something important I could tell Pa and the others.

"Go ahead and talk," I said. "But I'm not lowering the gun."

"Fair enough."

John turned away from me, and looked at his data-com. "While we've been talking, my data-com has been analyzing the musical language of these floating creatures. I think I can now initiate communications with them."

"No need for your data-com, John."

I started singing to a Floater, a pink one. I could tell by the way she flickered that she was bursting with curiosity.

I spoke with her, *Greetings, She-Who-Is-Curious. What do you want to know?*

The Floater came closer to me and sang back. *Greetings, She-Who-Is-Holding-A-Gun-On-A-Man, who is the man? Is he your enemy? Do you plan to kill him? Would you like me to kill him for you?*

Floaters were electricity-based creatures who could kill with a powerful bolt of lightning. I decided to decline her kind offer.

He is He-Who-Is-From-The-Empire. He is an enemy. However, I have decided not to kill him until he's given me certain information that would be useful to know. Please, do not kill him, the task has been assigned to me.

As you wish, She-Who-Will-Kill-When-She-Has-Certain-Information. He-Who-Is-From-The-Empire is attempting to speak with me using his machine. Shall we listen to what he has to say?

Yes, but speak in the human language so he can better understand you.

Very well.

CHAPTER FOUR

——— ● ———

JOHN

The girl, Amy, began to speak with one of the Floaters in a musical language. I watched the data-com closely and could follow the conversation, sort of. It appeared that these two were friends, and were deciding not to kill me now, but wait until later.

I thought back to my experience on Rhea V, when I had almost been sacrificed at the altar of the native species' fertility god. If I could talk my way out of that situation, I could talk myself out of this situation too.

But I was surprised when the Floater addressed me in English: "Greetings, He-Who-Comes-From-The-Empire. What is your business on this world and why does She-Who-Is-Holding-A-Gun-On-A-Man say you are an enemy?"

I wasn't sure what to say.

"Greet her back," said Amy, who still had the gun trained on me. "And make sure to get her name right."

"What is her name?" I asked.

"That depends on the situation," said Amy. "Right now she's asking you a question, so make sure to reference that in the name you call her."

"What if I get her name wrong?"

"She's waiting patiently, but her patience won't last forever. Figure out her name and speak to her."

As a Scout I had successfully initiated contact with two sentient species. I thought things through. "Greetings, She-Who-Waits-Patiently-While-The-Man-Thinks-About-What-To-Name-Her, my business on this world is exploration and, despite what she may have told you, I am not an enemy to She-Who-Is-Holding-A-Gun-On-A-Man."

Amy gave me a thumbs up and the Floater's bright glow got a bit brighter. But then the creature said, "You are He-Who-Is-From-The-Empire, are you not?"

"I am."

The Floater grew dim. "Your answer confuses me."

My mind was racing, then it occurred to me that this creature needed more than a simple affirmation.

"Excuse me, She-Who-Asks-Me-Questions, my answer was incomplete. I am He-Who-Is-From-The-Empire but I am also He-Who-Comes-In-Peace."

Amy snorted at this. The Floater's light flickered with disapproval. Neither of them believed I had come in peace.

"You will be escorted into the presence of She-Who-Decides," said the Floater. "She-Who-Is-Holding-A-Gun-On-A-Man, we wish you to attend as well."

Amy seemed reluctant.

"If I go with you," she said, "there's no way I'll be home before tomorrow morning. He-Who-Begat-Me would be furious."

"Can't you call him on your data-com and explain what's happening?" I asked.

Before Amy could respond, the Floater hovered closer. "We will send She-Who-Will-Carry-A-Message to He-Who-Begat-She-Who-Is-Holding-A-Gun-On-A-Man and explain the importance of the situation. Please, both of you, hop on the back of She-Who-Is-About-To-Carry-He-Who-Is-From-The-Empire-And-She-Who-Is-Holding-A-Gun-On-A-Man so we can see She-Who-Decides."

"This language takes some getting used to, Amy," I said.

"Let's just do what she says and go see She-Who-Decides."

"That's fine, but really, please put away your gun. It makes me nervous."

"Fine."

Amy put the gun away.

CHAPTER FIVE

———— ● ————

AMY

John hopped on the back of the Floater and I got on behind him. There was no way to grab a hold of the Floater so I grabbed John instead. The Floater immediately plunged downward and we fell into the mist.

John gave out a shout of delight as we zoomed through the air. Why was he enjoying himself when he knew I had orders to kill him? Maybe, John didn't take me seriously. Maybe, Pa should have sent a man to do this job, not a fourteen-year-old girl. But then, I remembered, Pa had married Ma when she was fourteen, which wasn't unusual in the colony. Pa didn't think of me as a girl, like an off-worlder would, he considered me a full-grown woman. People had to grow up fast on a colony as remote as ours. I was determined that I would not let Pa down. After we were done talking to She-Who-Decides, I would do the job Pa had given me and kill John.

We burst through the layer of mist and I could see the Valley below. The "People of the Valley" as we colonists called them, had no cities, villages, or even houses to live in. They did not cultivate the land, or dig mines, or cut down the forests. They had no roads. In fact, there were no signs of civilization to be seen because the People lived off the land of the Valley without altering it more than was absolutely necessary.

"Where are they?" John asked. No doubt he was realizing that the species he was about to meet might be sentient, but he would have to keep an open mind about what that meant.

"You will see when we land."

The Floater stopped when it was two meters above the ground, and we hopped off. John looked around. "I expected a welcoming party," he said. I realized to John's eyes there was nothing here but rocks and trees, and of course, Floaters. I knew the truth. I pointed at something that looked like a tree, but had no leaves. "That's a Walker," I said. "A Walker has arms and legs, and is the part of the People who hunts and gathers. Its brain is the size of a walnut, and it is non-sentient."

"OK."

"The boulders are the Minds. They are the brains, the intelligence of the People. But you can't detect their brains with a scanner, it's dissolved into the essence of the boulder. The Minds are deaf, dumb and blind, and must rely on the Floaters."

"OK."

"And you've already met the Floaters. They're the eyes and ears and mouths of the Minds. But they are completely mindless themselves. The Minds use electrical signals to control them."

"Are these your names for them, or their own."

"We colonists call them Walkers, Minds and Floaters. They call themselves and us names that depend on the situation, as you've already seen."

"Where is She-Who-Decides?"

"She's the big Mind over there," I pointed to a mound of boulders thirty meters away. "Let's walk over to her and greet her."

"But if the Floaters are the ones we communicate with, why was it necessary to come down here to see She-Who-Decides personally?"

"Why does the Empress meet people at the Palace personally when she could always have a data-com conversation?"

"I see your point."

John and I walked over to She-Who-Decides.

CHAPTER SIX

JOHN

I approached the mound of boulders named She-Who-Decides, and bowed with the respect due to the leader of a newly contacted native sentient race.

"Greetings, She-Who-Decides, I am He-Who-Comes-From-The-Empire, here on behalf of She-Who-Rules-The-Empire. I hope that this will be the beginning of a long era of peace and friendship between your people and mine."

There was a pause of nearly ten seconds. Then the Mind spoke, with the musical voice of a nearby Floater.

"Is there reason to believe, He-Who-Greets-She-Who-Decides, that there would ever *not* be peace and friendship between We-Who-Live-In-The-Valley and Those-Who-Conquer-The-Stars-But-The-Stars-Are-Not-Enough-They-Want-The-Worlds-Too?"

"Of course not." I lied, but then cursed myself for falling into an obvious trap.

"White man speak with forked tongue," the girl said. "I've already told She-Who-Decides the truth about the human race's less than stellar record when it encounters native sentient races on worlds it wishes to colonize — the

Hinni of Artania, rounded up and forced to live on reservations, the Aurox of Bella, enslaved and exploited, the Gui of Sheng, exterminated. I'm sure if I checked the historical records, I could find other examples."

"I must admit that She-Who-Betrays-Her-Own-Kind has a point," I said, angered with Amy and determined to defend the human race from her accusations. "We humans have much in our past to be ashamed of, but we have made enormous strides in learning from our mistakes and are fixed in our resolve to do better in the future. The Hinni now enjoy the full benefits afforded the human citizens of the Empire. The Aurox have been freed from slavery and are also citizens. Even our robots and clones have rights, not as many as humans, but we are making progress. And, you may be pleased to know, She-Who-Decides, that the Imperial Senate has recently passed a law saying that if a native sentient race is discovered on a world, that world is off-limits for human colonization."

Amy narrowed her eyes. "What happens if the Empire arrives on a world and discovers that a human colony already shares that world with a native sentient species?"

I turned to the girl, surprised by the question. "You already know the answer, Amy. Isn't that the reason you were sent by your colony to kill me?"

She barely moved, but once again the gun was in her hand, aimed at me.

"Let's pretend I don't know the answer, John. Explain it so even a stupid farm girl like me can understand."

CHAPTER SEVEN

---●---

AMY

I didn't want to kill John in front of She-Who-Decides, so my move, pulling out my gun again, was a bluff. But John didn't know that, or at least, I hoped not.

His reaction was not what I expected. "If you're going to shoot me Amy, shoot me. If not, put the gun away. All you're doing is pissing me off."

"Answer my question," I said. "What happens to our colony if you report that there is a native species on this world?"

Before I could respond, the Mind spoke. "Please, She-Who-Is-Holding-A-Gun-On-A-Man-Once-More, become once again She-With-An-Empty-Hand. She-Who-Decides does not want there to be violence amongst us at this moment, even if we decide that He-Who-Comes-From-The-Empire must die today."

That got John's attention. "Why would She-Who-Decides decide that He-Who-Comes-From-The-Empire must die today?"

"The answer is beneath your feet, He-Who-Comes-From-The-Empire," said the Mind. "Look around the Valley of the People and tell me what you see."

"What am I looking for?" John asked me. I reached down, picked a small rock off the ground, and tossed it to him.

"I don't get it," he said.

"There's dirt clinging to it," I said. "Clean it."

John took the stone and wiped it against the leg of his brown Scouting Service uniform. It was shiny, it was —

"Gold," he said, awe in his voice. "This is a nugget of gold."

"So, it is," I said. "Look around again."

He looked around. "Oh my God, these nuggets are everywhere."

"The Valley," I told him, "has gold nuggets scattered on the ground over thousands and thousands of square kilometers. Also, there's veins of gold that extend kilometers deep into the walls of the Valley. Pa has done a mineral survey, and estimates that the Valley has more gold than the Spanish Empire possessed at the height of its power in the seventeenth century, when galleons full of gold bullion coins made regular trips between the New World and Europe."

"But if there's that much gold on this world," asked John, "it must be nearly worthless to you. Why did you take my gold coins as payment?"

"We colonists only have the small amounts of gold the People give us in trade for our sugar. We do not come down into the Valley to take it for ourselves. We understand human nature. If we start taking the gold, our greed will get the better of us and we will not stop. We would force the People into slavery to dig it for us, and ultimately, the People would be destroyed."

"So, you're telling me that you have made the decision to leave all the gold alone, because you are good and kind people who don't want to exploit a native sentient race?"

John didn't seem convinced. I wanted to explain, but She-Who-Decides spoke first. "He-Who-Comes-From-The-Empire," she said. "She-With-An-Empty-Hand has told us you are a scientist, not an economist, but you have already guessed at the truth. If Those-Who-Share-Our-World-In-Peace dug up all the gold in the Valley, it would do them no good. Gold is not like water, something you must have. You cannot eat gold, or drink it, or use it to build things. Gold only has value when people think it has value, and to have value, it must be scarce. Gold that is too plentiful becomes worthless. Do you understand?"

"Yes, I think so." John said, no doubt wondering how She-Who-Decides had picked up such knowledge.

"Then," She-Who-Decides continued, "you must also understand what would happen if your Empire were to learn of the gold in our Valley. While the gold is too plentiful to have value for one human colony, it is not too plentiful to have value in a vast interstellar Empire that uses gold as its currency. There would be a gold rush. Millions of humans would come to our world, dig up the gold in the Valley, and We-Who-Live-In-The-Valley would be trampled over and destroyed."

"But, She-Who-Decides, I was trying to explain that would *not* happen. Under Imperial law, if a world is inhabited by a native sentient race, humans are prohibited from colonizing that world. When I report to the Empire that an illegal human colony has established itself on this world, the Empire will order the colony to be evacuated. So, you see — "

Without thinking, I pulled out my gun again and pointed it at John. "You will evacuate our colony? Not without a fight."

John turned to me with an unperturbed expression. It annoyed me that nothing I said or did scared him. He gave my hand a karate chop, and the gun went flying out of my fingers. I grabbed my hand and winced in pain.

"You're too big to spank, Amy," he said. "But I will beat you senseless if you point a gun at me again."

She-Who-Decides said. "She-Who-Just-Got-A-Gun-Knocked-Out-Of-Her-Hand, I have asked you to refrain from displays of violence during these negotiations. If you cannot respect my wishes, withdraw so He-Who-Comes-From-The-Empire and I can have a civilized discussion."

"I'm sorry," I said. "I'll be good." But I wasn't sorry one little bit. When Pa had given me the mission to kill this man, he had told me it was to save the People of the Valley. Now, I realized that I had to kill him to save our colony. We had lived on this world one hundred years. What gave the Empire the right to force us to leave?

CHAPTER EIGHT

JOHN

We slept that night on the floor of the Valley of the People. The next morning, a Floater took us back up. I jumped down and started walking back to my camp. Amy jumped down after me and followed. She-Who-Decides had given me Amy's gun, so I wasn't afraid the colonist girl would shoot me in the back. But she remained dangerous, and if she decided to, she could fetch more colonists to help her complete her mission to kill me. I had to convince her that my way was the right way.

I turned around and confronted her. "Amy, you're going to have to see reason."

"Reason? Is that what you call it? You want me to stand by while you report our colony to the Empire? Then you want me to go quietly as the Marines force us out of our homes and take us to some re-settlement camp? How is that reasonable?"

"Your colony never got a Charter, which means it's illegal. You never had the right to colonize this world."

"Who says?"

"The Empire."

"Why should we care about what the Empire thinks? We're thousands of light-years away from the edge of Known Space. The Empire doesn't even know our colony exists and will continue not knowing we exist unless you report us. So, why do you have to report us?"

"It's my job."

"So, what would happen if you didn't do your job, just this one time?"

"If I didn't report you, it would only delay the inevitable," I said. "When I entered orbit, my ship started scanning the surface of this world and all that information was stored in my ship's computer. Every time I used my hand scanner, the information was transmitted in real time to my ship's computer. The computer knows there is a human colony on this world and also knows there's a native sentient species. Even if I don't report you, the Empire will learn of this situation when the information in my computer is uploaded to the Weave. That will happen the first time I dock in a space station or at the starport of a civilized world. I'm sorry, but even if I agree to keep your colony a secret, you will be found out eventually anyway."

"You could hack the ship's computer, John. Delete all information about this world."

"That would require the skills of a top hacker, and I'm only so-so. Also, I'm not going to risk it. I would spend at least five years in a penal colony if I was caught, and I *would* get caught. I might be able to delete all information about your world, but there would be unexplained empty spaces, hints that information had been removed. They would flag security, and I would be interrogated. Eventually, I would talk and tell them all about your colony."

"You don't get it, John," Amy said, her teeth clenched. "This world is my home. Your Empire has no right to come busting in and forcing us to leave. Why can't you get that?"

"Because, Amy, I believe in something bigger than the fate of one human colony. I believe that humans don't have the right to move onto some other sentient species' world and shove them aside or exploit them. The People were here first and this is their world. You and the other colonists will have to find some other place to live."

"But you heard what She-Who-Decides said. She doesn't want you to report this world either. She believes that if the Empire finds out about this world, with all its gold, humans will come here and destroy them. If you won't listen to me, listen to her."

We were just about to reach the camp. I could see the outlines of my Scout ship through the trees.

"Amy, I will admit that we humans have a long history of breaking promises to native peoples, but I believe this time, it will be different. We've taken great strides in our moral progress and —"

I realized there was a glowing red dot on my chest. I stopped. Amy stopped behind me.

Just as I realized that, two more dots appeared.

Then ten more.

"Dr. Carver," it was a man's voice. "We are not inclined to be violent men. But if you try to run or twitch so much as a pinky finger towards your pistol, we will drill you with so many holes your body will look like a burned out life support filter."

"Pa!" Amy ran forward into the camp, got between me and their laser sights.

I ran into the woods.

CHAPTER NINE

——— ● ———

AMY

As I ran toward Pa's voice, I heard a popping noise. Something slammed into my shoulder and I fell down hard. There were more popping noises, and I heard bullets whizzing over my head. Pa yelled, "Cease fire, damn you! Cease fire!"

"He's getting away!" said a man's voice.

"Don't shoot him, fellas," Pa said. "Just chase after him and catch him if you can."

"He's a Scout, Mr. Branagan," said another man's voice. "Surviving in the wilderness is what he's been trained to do. We may never catch him."

"You definitely won't catch him if you stand here yapping at me," Pa said. "Go out there and get him."

I was flat on my back, staring upwards towards the sky. I saw Pa, leaning down to me, smiling kindly as he always did with me and everyone else.

"I couldn't kill him, Pa," I said. "I had more than one chance but I couldn't kill him."

Someone had handed Pa a piece of cloth and he was using it to press down on my shoulder to staunch the bleeding.

"I know Amy, it was unfair to even ask you to do this. But anyone else wouldn't even had gotten near him. Scouts and illegal colonists have been mortal enemies for as far long back as anyone remembers. You were the only one I could send in who he wouldn't have shot on sight."

"You could have just had a sniper take him out."

"I could, but remember, killing him was our last resort. I told you to talk to him first, see if you could persuade him that reporting this colony to the Empire was bad for everyone on this world, we humans, and the People of the Valley. Did you make any progress?"

"No, he's so damn sure he's right he didn't listen to anything we said. We told him there'd be a gold rush, and the People would be destroyed, but he thinks humans have learned their lesson, and all those horrible things humans have done in the past will never happen again."

Two men arrived with a blanket they had jury-rigged into a stretcher, and they put me on it.

"Pa," I said. "Please make sure no one kills him. If anyone gets to kill him, it should be me. I've put up with his garbage for two days, so I've earned the right to kill him."

"OK, Amy," Pa said. "But try not to hate him. From his point of view, everything he believes is perfectly reasonable."

The men lay me down in the bed of a truck, and they drove me off to the clinic.

CHAPTER TEN

—— ◖ ——

JOHN

I watched from the perch of a tree, twenty meters above the ground. The old one, Pa, milled about in my camp a bit, then he and three other men started messing around with my ship. They were working on the other side, so I couldn't see clearly what was happening. I decided to climb down, move stealthily through the trees to the other side of the ship, and climb up another tree. With men and dogs searching for me, it took me three hours to get to where I was going. When I arrived at my new perch, I saw what they were doing: attacking my fuel tank with a mining drill.

I would have been within my rights to kill them, but I had no wish to declare war against an entire colony of thousands of people with no one to call for back-up. Stunning them would have been just as bad, I would be discovered and shot. So I waited impatiently while they bore a hole through the hull and drained out the water that Scout ships use as fuel.

At the end of the day, the men went home, not even leaving a guard. They knew my ship was crippled. I could not fly away until I had re-patched the hole and filled the tank again, a job that would take hours. I climbed down, moved stealthily to my ship, and entered the ship through the airlock. The lock was thumbprint coded so only I could get in.

I went to the bridge and checked the fuel gauge, which was solidly to the left indicating empty. There might be enough fuel in the lines to get into orbit, but then my engine would sputter and die. I had no way to leave this world at this time.

But I could get out a distress signal. It was a long shot, but the life of a Scout was a series of long shots that paid off. I checked the navigation system, and saw that my journey to this world traced through fourteen wormholes. If I traced the path backwards, it led to Navai, a frontier world, but within the borders of the Empire. If I sent my distress signal down that path, eventually word would get to the Scouting Service that I was alive and in need of rescue. It took me an hour to do the numbers, but finally I was ready to push the button that would send the signal. If my calculations were correct, it would take two years for the signal to reach Navai, and, if they sent someone right away, three years or so for a rescue ship to arrive. Five years, all told.

I could survive in the wilderness for five years, that was not a problem. Scouts often lost their ships and had to survive with nothing more than a knife. But was I willing to live such a life, isolated and in constant danger of being eaten by predators? I realized there was no need. Once I had sent the signal, I would surrender to the colonists. Amy might want to kill me, but I figured her Pa would be more reasonable and realize there was no rational reason to kill me since I had already sent the distress signal and the Empire was on its way.

But then I thought, what if rescue doesn't come? The Empire was locked in a life-and-death struggle with the alien race Zetti, who kept human slaves and feasted on their flesh. Most men of military age had been drafted to fight this war, which is why the Scouting Service was recruiting boys to carry on its exploration mission. I had been recruited at the age of fifteen, trained in one year, and had been in the field for a year. At the age of seventeen, I was a hardened veteran. But would the Empire divert valuable resources to rescue one Scout thousands of light-years beyond its borders?

I had to be sure, and the only way was to give the Empire a reason to come. I plugged in my hand scanner and looked at the information I had gathered. I widened the bandwidth of the distress signal and attached the information that showed that an illegal human colony was located on a world with a native sentient race. This was a clear violation of Imperial law that would require that a contingent of Marines be sent along with a transport big enough to evacuate the colony. I was about to press the button that would send the signal when a dark thought crowded into the back of my mind. It would not be enough. In peacetime, action would be taken. But during a war, a mission to evacuate a colony might have such a low priority it would never reach the authorization stage, and I would not be rescued. I realized I had to add additional incentive for the Empire to come rescue me.

I thought about the gold. The conversation I had with She-Who-Decides indicated more gold was in the Valley of the People than the Spanish Empire had ever possessed even at their height of power. She might have been exaggerating, but I thought that was improbable. If I told the Empire about the gold, I thought, they would send a fleet and Marines, not to exploit it, but to secure it to make certain such a vast source of wealth did not fall into the wrong hands.

That's what I told myself. And I justified myself further when I considered that if my ship had not been crippled, and I had left this world, the Empire would have found out about the gold anyway.

The human race was different now, I believed. We've learned from the mistakes of the past. Even if the Empire decided to mine the gold, they would make sure the People of the Valley were not harmed in the process.

I loaded the information about the gold onto the distress signal and pushed the button. I let it broadcast for fifteen seconds, then turned it off. Typically, a distress signal broadcasts indefinitely, but I had to be satisfied that a fifteen second burst would be enough to alert the Empire of my presence on this world. Any longer, and the colonists would definitely find me out.

Now that I had done it, I realized that Amy must never know. I had been careful not to show fear as she threatened me with her laser pistol numerous times over the past two days. But I had lied when I told her she didn't have the look of a killer. She did. I knew she hadn't ever killed a human, but that made her more dangerous, not less.

I left the ship, locked it, and started walking in the direction of the colony's largest settlement. The walk would take four hours, giving me plenty of time to prepare all the lies I would have to tell.

CHAPTER ELEVEN

JOHN

My surrender was without incident and I was swiftly integrated into the colony. They offered me a job teaching mathematics and science at the school. I took it, then leased a small apartment in town.

At first, I was horrified when I learned Amy's true age was fourteen, making my thoughts about her uncomfortable and inappropriate. Why had she lied to me? This wasn't a small lie, it was the kind of lie that could get a man in a lot of trouble. But, after thinking about it, I decided to let it go.

Amy and I decided to be friends, and as we got older our friendship blossomed as she discovered that I was a good listener. Also, I was far more interesting to talk to then the other men of the colony, who talked about the crops, and the weather, and how the weather affected the crops. I loaned her my books, and then we would discuss them into the wee hours of the morning. I did not ever touch her, though I knew she wanted me to. When she was sixteen, we agreed to initiate a romantic, but non-sexual relationship. Pa approved of us as a couple, and that was enough for everyone, since everyone loved Pa and respected his opinions. We were married a week after she turned eighteen, and I was the ripe old age of twenty-one. The colonists built us a house the same day, and we moved in. That night, we finally made love. I would like to say the years of waiting made it better, but neither one of us knew what we were doing. But it didn't take long before we figured things out, and then she was insatiable.

The only hitch was the screaming incident. One day she woke up screaming. I tried everything I could do to comfort her, but every time I touched her, she reacted with violence. The doctor came and tried to give her sedatives, but after taking them, she spit them out. She was thrashing about the house, knocking things down and hurting herself. Finally, the doctor and I, with the help of Pa, wrapped her in three thick woolen blankets and fastened them down with duct tape. She kept on screaming, but at least she couldn't hurt herself.

This went on for a week. I was concerned because we couldn't get any food down her throat, and we had to use a funnel and hose to force down water. I was afraid she might die of thirst or malnutrition.

But then came the morning when she woke up, and with an annoyed expression, said, "John, why the hell am I tied up like this?"

She had no memory of anything she'd done, anything that had happened. I untied her, and strangely enough, our lives went on as if nothing had happened.

In the back of my mind, I thought about the distress signal. I had never had to lie, no one had asked if I sent a distress signal. But I knew I was on borrowed time. The day would come when the Empire would arrive, wanting its gold, and Amy would learn the truth that I had betrayed her, the colony, and the People of the Valley. I was scared, because I had no clue what the hell she might do.

CHAPTER TWELVE

———— ⬤ ————

AMY

Five years had passed since John had arrived. One day, the nurse at the clinic informed me I was having a baby. The next day, I found out that the Empire had arrived. I knew right away that John had caused the first of these events. It was only later that John admitted he had also caused the second.

All I knew at the time was that my world was ending.

I was standing in front of the fountain in Founder's Circle when a shadow passed over me. I looked up, and saw a man falling from the sky on the end of a parachute. I turned to my friend, an unmarried young woman, and said: "Hide." She didn't argue, but turned to run. I, the daughter of the town's unofficial leader, decided to stay and try to find out what was happening.

The man landed on the street and unhitched himself from the parachute, which blew away with the wind. He was armored head to toe, and carried large objects which I assumed were weapons. He took no notice of me, though I was standing only ten meters away from him. He started to talk, though not to me. I couldn't make out what he was saying, it was military jargon. But the gist of it was, he had landed safely, there was no hostile activity in his sector, and he awaited further orders.

The orders came back, stay where you are, report in every five minutes.

You may have surmised from reading thus far that I was quite wild at the age of fourteen. At the age of nineteen, I was slightly less rambunctious, but I was still a woman determined not to be ignored when a stranger dropped into my town uninvited.

"Hello, sir?" I said to the man. I recognized the insigna on his right arm as matching the flag John had planted at his camp all those years ago. He was from the Empire, then. Good to know.

He did not acknowledge me, but walked around Founder's Circle, looking for an enemy to shoot perhaps.

I walked up to the man, got in his face, and waved my arms.

"Hello, sir? I'm talking to you."

I could not see his face as it was behind a one-way visor, but he seemed startled to see me. He pushed a button on his arm, and the visor turned transparent. I could see that inside the suit was a very young man, little more than a boy. He stared at me, not knowing at first what to make of me, then said: "Miss, this is a combat zone. All civilians are ordered to return to their homes and stay in place until the emergency is over."

"Who is giving the orders?" I demanded. "Why is this a combat zone? What emergency are you talking about?"

The boy obviously had no idea what to say to me. But he was saved when another armored man strolled up and addressed me.

"Miss," he said. I could tell he was a much older man. He had more stripes on his arm which I knew indicated he was one of the higher ranks of enlisted men. "Miss, it is not safe for you to be here out on the street. Please, go home."

"I won't move a muscle until you explain to me why you hooligans are here, and why you think you have the right to order people around."

I wished that I had remembered to wear my pistol that morning.

Pa, in his apron, arrived at that moment, huffing and puffing. It was a chilly day, but his body was coated with sweat. He had run all the way from the inn where he worked, three blocks away.

"Amy, you'll be the death of me." Pa grabbed my arm and started pulling me away from the men in armor. "Leave these men alone. They're busy right now and don't have time to answer all your ridiculous questions."

I was furious.

"This is our home, Pa. These men have no right to come here, wave around their weapons, and order us around."

"Amy," Pa pleaded with me, "you are putting us all in grave danger provoking these men. Come with me at once, or I will pick you up and carry you."

Then I saw John, in the suit he wore at his teacher's job. He said nothing to me — just shook his head with disbelief or disapproval, I never knew which. He punched me in the face and knocked me out cold.

CHAPTER THIRTEEN

JOHN

Maximillan MacKensie, the Fourth, wore a big white cowboy hat and greeted me with a big toothy smile. He wore a white silk shirt with ruffles at the collar, blue jeans, a leather vest, and alligator boots. He was positioned at the head of a long table in a conference room at the Crossarms Inn, the only conference room in town in the only inn in town. Also in attendence were six other men and two women, all in gray business suits. Max shouted, "Here's the man of the hour!" as I entered the room, and the assembled suits applauded.

He slapped me on the back with manly vigor, handed me a cigar, and lit it. The other men and women greeted me with handshakes, and one of the women, a very attractive young brunette, slipped me a piece of paper which turned out to be her data-com number. I was somewhat taken aback by all the positive attention, but so far, no one had clued me in as to what the hell this was all about.

But I knew. It was the gold.

All the worst things I had feared would happen, had happened. Marines had dropped in and seized control of the entire colony. More Marines had landed in the Valley, and were securing positions at every strategic location, Heavy shuttles were landing, dropping off men, robots, machines and equipment.

Max was running the three ring circus, and I was his favorite trick pony.

He told me his life story, how he had made his fortune constructing fuel refineries in orbit around gas giants, then went on to purchase a failing tri-vi conglomerate and turned it around, then bought up low priced buildings in Hun Wat's Lower City and doubling their value with renovations and improved security. I pretended to be interested, and while he talked we had a very good steak dinner and all the bourbon we could drink.

I got drunk. The brunette who had given me her number sidled up to me, and the next thing I knew we were in her room. I'm not sure what happened after that, but you can take a wild guess and you'd probably be right.

CHAPTER FOURTEEN

———●———

AMY

John stumbled in at three in the morning, stinking of booze. I was sitting on the couch in the living room, patiently like a predator cat, setting up an ambush. He saw what was happening, but sat down anyway, in his big easy chair. He knew, there was no way to avoid this. Might as well get it over with. One thing I admired about my husband, he never backed down even when I was aiming a gun at his head.

"I sent a distress signal," John said. "You can't blame me for that. I was a Scout who had lost my ship on a hostile world. You can't blame me for sending a distress signal."

I said nothing. As I expected, my silence unnerved him, and he gushed words to fill the gap.

"It was more than a distress signal, but you can't blame me for that either."

This time I spoke. My voice was gentle, kind even. I was the perfect picture of the understanding wife.

"How was it more than a distress signal, John?"

"I increased the bandwidth," he said.

"I don't know what that means, John."

"I widened the signal so it could carry more bits of data per microsecond."

"I still don't understand, John."

"I made the signal bigger so I could tell the Empire more about what was happening on the colony."

"That I understand," I said. "You told the Empire that our colony was illegal, and that we should not be here on a world inhabited by native sentient life forms."

"Yes."

I laid down my trap.

"I forgive you, John."

"What?"

"You are a man who sticks to his principles. I disagree with what you did, it will mean our colony will have to relocate, but I can't condemn you for doing what you believed was right. In fact, I admire you for what you did. Now, the People of the Valley will be safe from us humans, forever. I realize that that is the reason I love you, that you always do what you believe is right. Please John, don't ever change. Always do what you believe is right, even if I and everyone else in the universe is against you. Can you promise me that?"

"What?"

"Promise me, you'll always do the right thing."

I could almost hear the wheels turning in his head. He had seen the trap for what it was. But I expected that, the trap was so obvious. He'd be the biggest fool in the universe if he believed that I believed anything I had just said. What was his next move?

"Our world is ending, Amy, and all you want to do is play your stupid mind games."

"I really am angry with you, John."

"I come in, expecting to have a big confrontation because I betrayed your colony and the People of the Valley.

That's what would happen if you were a normal woman with normal feelings and then you would forgive me or not forgive me and our marriage would end or not end, but at least we'd be normal."

"You wanted normal? No, you didn't. You married the crazy girl who almost shot you three times on the day we met. I admired the way you stood up to me, but you must have been shitting your pants the whole time, realizing I might just end you. If you wanted normal, you should never have married me."

"I suppose that's true."

"It is."

"On the day we met, your crazy made you cute. You waved that little gun around and I thought, she's cute. You're right, I was unsure whether I'd survive the day, but I knew that showing fear would be the worst thing I could do. So I brazened it out, and you didn't shoot me."

"You were afraid of me, then, but brazened it out."

"Yes."

"I thought, this man is a Scout, and has faced death so many times and has survived so many dangerous situations, that a girl with a gun doesn't even faze him."

"That was the impression I was trying to make."

"But you were afraid."

"Yes. I lied when I said you didn't have the eyes of a killer. You did. And you do."

I pulled out my gun and aimed it at him.

As he had on that first day, he showed no fear. But now, I knew the truth. He had been afraid of me on that first day, and he was afraid of me now.

"Amy, we have serious issues to discuss. Max has given every colonist, including us, thousands of shares in his company that has obtained from the Empire the rights to extract all the gold in the Valley. Even using conservative estimates of how much gold there is, we will all be billionaires many times over."

"You are still putting on the pretense that you do not fear me. Why?"

"Amy, put away the gun. I'm not going to tell you again —"

I pressed the trigger of the laser pistol and sliced off his left leg, just below the knee. He howled with pain.

"I told you I was angry, but you don't listen."

I sliced off John's right leg, just below the knee.

The front door burst open and Pa came in with a shotgun.

I saw in his face what he was about to do. What he felt he had to do.

"I'm sorry, baby girl. This is a problem I should have dealt when you were four and I caught you torturing that puppy with a rusty screwdriver."

He aimed his shotgun at my head, ready to blow it off. But he loved me, and that made him hesitate.

Big mistake. I pressed the trigger and sliced the beam, cutting Pa clean in half.

But Pa had distracted me. Now, John had his laser pistol out. But he loved me, and that made him hesitate.

Stupid men. I rotated the power dial to one hundred percent, so I could give my husband a blast that would vaporize him, the chair he sat in, and punch a hole in the wall behind.

I pulled the trigger, and nothing happened.

I had forgotten. If you asked a laser pistol to give your shot more power than it had in its battery, it gave you no power at all. I was sure that a man had made this stupid design decision. A woman would have known that power is malleable, never an all or nothing proposition.

John's hand was steady, and I could see my death written in his eyes. This time, he would shoot me. And I would die.

But then, I had a thought. "I'm pregnant with your child."

In all the chaos, I had forgotten to give him this news. Now, it had the impact I desired. He lowered his aim, for a moment. It was all the time I needed. I leaped off the couch, over the glass-topped coffee table, and hit him in the midriff with a full-body tackle. The springs of the easy chair creaked in protest and we all fell backwards — me, John, and the chair. The laser pistol flew out of his hand, and I scrambled after it as it slid across the tile floor.

I was invigorated, knowing my life was on the hair-trigger. Only one of us would come out of this alive.

CHAPTER FIFTEEN

───◖───

JOHN

My wife had gone certifiably insane, and if I lived though the next few seconds, I would count myself blessed.

I had expected drama when I admitted to her I had told the Empire about the gold in my distress signal, sent in a fifteen second burst five years ago. To save myself from a life stranded on this colony world, I had put everyone in danger. Now, my worst nightmares had been realized. A wealthy trillionaire had arrived, and had already begun work strip-mining the Valley.

My wife's reaction was not what I wanted, but I should have expected it. She pulled her laser pistol on me, and sliced off both my legs. Now, we were wrestling on the floor. My laser pistol was lying on the tiles, just centimeters from her grasping fingertips. I was grabbing her legs to pull her back.

In my short career as a Scout I had fought many dangerous beasts on untamed worlds, but none were as dangerous as my wife. I had the advantage of strength and superior fighting skill, but she was ruthless, which gave her the edge. That fact was driven home for me when she clawed at my face, and with sharp fingernails ripped out my eye. She cackled with glee, and I realized she was enjoying herself as she pulled and sliced me apart, piece by piece.

I had to end it, fast. I had no legs, but I still had upper-body strength. I grabbed the glass top of the coffee table with both hands, and using all the power in my arms, I picked it up and smashed it on my wife's head. The glass shattered, sending jagged shards in every direction. Some of these shards lodged into my body, but I could not stop to feel the pain. She was beyond all reason, so I had to be beyond all reason too. I picked up a glass shard and stabbed desperately at my wife's neck, hoping to sever a jugular vein. I got lucky and severed her windpipe instead. Dark red fluid started bubbling out of her neck, she was drowning in her own blood. She was doomed to die in moments, but she was not finished, not by a long shot. She picked up a shard, grabbed my arm, and severed the vein in my wrist. Then, while I stared at my wrist dumbfounded, she severed the vein in my other wrist. Now, I was bleeding out of both veins, and I would die too. At this moment, it didn't matter much to me who would die first. But it mattered to her. She took that shard and drove it so deep in my neck the point came out the other side. Then she lay down and died.

I collapsed, and as the darkness hit me, I had one final thought:

I should have killed her the first time she drew a gun on me.

CHAPTER SIXTEEN

---◉---

CHARLES

Charles Hartmann, Jr., Vice-President of Public Relations at the MacKensie Mining Enterprises, alighted from the mini-shuttle and stepped out on the work site. It was located at the bottom of a deep chasm, the survey team had told him it was ten kilometers wide and fifteen kilometers deep. A robot handed him a hard-hat and he put it on. Charles believed that leaders should set an example. And the young executive considered himself a leader of the men and robots working here, even if he showed up only twice a week dressed inappropriately in tailored suits that cost twelve thousand dollars, and stayed only an hour before climbing back on the mini-shuttle and flying back to the comfort of headquarters.

The Chief Engineer approached and shook Charles' hand. The Chief's palms were covered with thick callouses, built up from decades of hard work, contrasting sharply with Charles' baby soft hands, indicating a life of comfortable office work. Both men noticed the difference, much to Charles' embarrassment.

Charles had come today on a fact-finding mission. The colonists were spreading rumors that a sentient race inhabited this valley, and the mining activity of the company was destroying their natural habitat. It was critically important to squash these rumors before they reached the Weave sheets or tri-vi broadcasts. The slightest hint that yet another sentient species was being brutalized at the hands of greedy humans would cause a scandal of interstellar proportions. The Empire would shut down the operation, and there would be investigations, inquiries, perhaps even subpoenas to appear before a Grand Jury. The public would be outraged, and there would be boycotts, letter campaigns, even death threats. Executives like Charles Hartmann, Jr. might be singled out for specific public condemnation. If things really got out of hand, Charles might be ejected from his country club. If there were any truth to the rumors that a sentient lifeform lived in this valley, Charles would recommend to the board that they should shut down the operation and take appropriate measures to ensure the sentient lifeforms were saved. Perhaps a relocation of the lifeforms to a natural preserve, or a zoo.

"Tell me, Chief," Charles said, "have you seen any sign of intelligence in any of the creatures you've observed in this valley? And please, keep in mind that we are dealing with life that is totally alien to anything we humans are familiar with. Intelligence may be demonstrated in ways so subtle, it would be difficult for us to discern them. Please, tell me if anything has been a little off — or even slightly unusual."

"Well, Mr. Hartmann, we had a bit of trouble with the trees. But we've dealt with it."

"What was the trouble?"

"They're not actually trees, they have no leaves, but they look like wooden stick-figures, and they started attacking our workers. We tried non-lethal solutions, like putting nets around the work-site, but the trees seemed determined to stop us."

"You said you dealt with it."

"Well, this went on for four weeks when Mr. MacKensie came to the site, said there had enough delays and money wasted dealing with the creatures, and he ordered the Marines to sweep through the valley and hit every tree with a flamethrower. And, it seems sad to see a whole species of life exterminated, but the problem was solved."

"Were the trees sentient?"

"Our xeno-biologists cut one open and discovered they had brains the size of walnuts. They couldn't have had more than animal-level intelligence. It is impossible, they told us, that sentient creatures could have brains that small."

"OK, well the company is guilty of showing utter contempt for this world's environment, but no sentient race was involved. Have you seen anything else unusual?"

"Well, now that you mention it, a few weeks after the trees were dealt with, we started having problems with the rocks."

"What kind of problems?"

"We didn't see them move or anything, but somehow they would always be in the way so we couldn't move a vehicle through an area, or place a piece of equipment or machinery. Perhaps our minds were playing tricks on us, because we would compare tri-vi images taken from day to day and the rocks were always in the same place. But —"

"But what, Chief?"

"They were always in the way."

"The rocks?"

"Yes."

"So what did you do to solve this problem?"

"We brought in heavy load lifters and put all the rocks in one pile. Then, we used explosives and power hammers to reduce the rocks into gravel. We plan to use the gravel as bedding material for the tracks we will build in the mine tunnels for the carts that transport the ore. So, problem solved."

"OK, I can't see anyone making a fuss over rocks. Tell me, what can you tell me about the Floaters? I hear they are brightly colored and make wonderful music as they float through the air. A delight to see and hear, I am told."

"They were, but I'm afraid I haven't seen a Floater in these parts for at least six months. They seemed to disappear about the same time we burned down all the trees and pounded all the rocks to rubble. A worker told me that they found a field full of dying Floaters, all pale and sickly, whimpering to themselves like they'd just given up hope or something."

"A tragic loss, but I've been assured the Floaters are not sentient."

"No, Mr. Hartmann, a Floater is a completely mindless creature. Our xeno-biologists never figured out how they functioned with not even the most rudimentary of brains."

"I suppose that's a mystery that won't ever be solved, now that they're gone."

"I suppose."

"Chief, we're mainly concerned with sentient life forms, but it sounds like the operation has already driven three non-sentient life forms into extinction. It seems a bit — careless. Please make an effort to avoid more extinctions."

"So long as a species of lifeform doesn't interfere with our operations, they'll have nothing to fear from us," said the Chief.

"Right — of course."

"Now, if you'll excuse me Mr. Hartmann, I have a lot of work to do and must get back to it."

The Chief shook Charles' hand and left him.

Charles watched the Chief's back as he walked away. The last part of that meeting hadn't gone right, somehow. The Chief's words had been — dismissive. But Charles was not the kind of man to force a confrontation when he felt slighted. He had accomplished what he had set out to do, determined for himself that these rumors of sentient life forms in the Valley were untrue. He would write a press release tonight, setting the record straight, and release it on the Weave in the morning. With any luck, the evening tri-vi broadcasts would pick it up, and then it would go viral.

Charles Hartmann, Jr., young executive with a bright future ahead of him, walked back to the mini-shuttle, climbed on board, and ordered the robot pilot to return to headquarters.

CHRISSY

DANDELION

CHAPTER ONE

———— ◯ ————

CHRISSY AND VIOLET

"I have the feeling I'm about to be the main character in a romance novel," Chrissy said, taking a bite from a crumpet.

"That's an odd thing to say," said her friend Violet, pouring herself another cup of tea, "though it's not even close to the oddest thing you've *ever* said."

Chrissy didn't ask Violet what the oddest thing she'd ever said was — she already knew and didn't want her friend to repeat the story. It was the time she had said that looking at her cat, Bellbottoms, licking herself made her feel flushed and warm inside. Violet had told the tale to everyone. Chrissy still could not figure out why she had said it.

"Don't change the subject," Chrissy said, "I want to talk about the here and now, not the past."

"OK, let's talk about your feeling — now — that you are — what? About to be the main character in a romance novel. How does it feel to feel that way?"

"Well, pleasant really. It gives me hope."

"Hope of what? You already have a man in your life, a certain Roger Roper of Pumpernickel Acres," said Violet.

"Everyone expects he will ask you to marry him any day now. It seems that if you are in a romance novel the book is almost finished, because soon you will have that 'happily ever after' that girls like us dream of."

"Will I?" Chrissy smiled.

Violet put her cup down, grabbed her friend's hand, and squeezed.

"There's something you're not telling me."

Chrissy wasn't sure she could trust Violet with her secret.

"Maybe — maybe not."

"Spill!"

"I have reason to believe Mr. Roper will ask me to marry him tonight at the Roper's Midsummer ball."

"And?"

"I will turn him down."

"No!"

"Yes!"

"So what will happen after that?"

"'He' will come to the ball tonight and introduce himself to me."

"Who?"

"The man I *will* marry, of course. The 'happily ever after' at the end of this story we're in."

"How can you be so sure?"

"I don't know *how* I know, I just know."

"Wow, Chrissy, that's insane."

"I know!"

The girls rushed through preparations for the ball. Both were giddy. Chrissy was eager to meet the new man in her life who would replace Mr. Roper. Violet, unbeknownst to

Chrissy, was eager to meet Mr. Roper after Chrissy turned down his marriage proposal, and be the first girl to set her claws into him.

But first, Chrissy's mother insisted they feast on leftover ham. She didn't want them to look unladylike by eating too much of the hors d'oeuvre at the ball.

"It occurs to me that if you are the main character of this romance novel," said Violet, "I'm the best friend."

"Yes, I did think about that."

"The best friend is supposed to be a bit quirky, isn't she?"

"Yes, I suppose."

"She is either not as attractive as the main character, or she's a bit overweight, or she's a colored servant girl, or secretly a lesbian."

"But none of that is true about you, Violet, so perhaps you're not my best friend after all."

"Oh my, Chrissy, that sounds so horrible," said Violet, "but it's true, I'm not really a good friend to you. Even now, I'm plotting to betray you."

Violet broke out in tears. Chrissy rushed over and kneeled beside her.

"Oh my dear sweet Violet, tell me, how could it possibly be true you're plotting to betray me?"

"After you turn down Mr. Roper's offer of marriage tonight, I was planning to throw myself at him shamelessly," said Violet. "I love him, Chrissy, I've always loved him. When you told me you were rejecting him, my heart leaped for joy."

Chrissy gave her friend a hug.

"You can have him, Violet, with my blessing. I hope, really I do, that you can find your own 'happily ever after' with Mr. Roper."

CHAPTER TWO

MR. ROPER AND MR. MOORE

The Ropers always gave the Mid-summer ball, and this year they outdid themselves. The food was top quality. The decorations were the most expensive possible. The musicians, imported from the continent, played the latest music numbers, and the young people danced for hour after hour as the older generation watched from the side lines with admiration and love. Chrissy danced with many, but Mr. Roper had priority, since he was her intended, or would be, until later tonight. Finally, came the moment she had expected ever since her spy in the Roper home had tipped her off this morning:

"Miss Dandelion," Mr. Roper said, "would you be so kind as to accompany me to the balcony?"

She realized she should be dreading this moment, but she was eager to get it over with. Only when she'd completed this task would she meet the man who would be her "happily ever after".

"Yes, Mr. Roper," she said. Together, they went through the French doors and outside.

It was a balmy summer evening. A full moon hung high in the sky, surrounded by thousands of twinkling stars. If

Chrissy had been in love with Mr. Roper, this would be the highlight of her life, a memory cherished through old age. But Chrissy had never been in love with him. Why she had allowed their relationship to continue for so long, and lead to this moment, she didn't know.

He took her hands in his: "Miss Dandelion," he started, "in the years we have known each other, I have become rather attached to you."

Chrissy was only half paying attention. Her eyes were sweeping the balcony, trying to determine whether any of the other men here was the man she expected to meet tonight.

"When we are apart, my heart aches for you."

A young couple were necking on the other end.

"I have come to believe that the only solution to this problem of us being apart and my heart aching for you, is to arrange our lives so that we no longer have to be apart."

A young man came into view, climbing up the stairs that led down into the gardens. He was tall, had a full head of dark hair, and dark eyes. He was wearing an ascot tie and a suit with trousers, a clothing style that was only now becoming the fashion with gentlemen. In one hand, he held a cigarette — another recent innovation. He took a puff while he watched Chrissy with smoldering eyes, and she *knew:*

This is the man.

Mr. Roper fumbled with something in his coat pocket — no doubt a ring. Chrissy couldn't wait any longer, she had to meet *the man.*

"No. I'm sorry Mr. Roper, but no."

Mr. Roper was confused, "No, *what?*"

"I know what you're about to ask me and the answer is 'no'."

"How could you possibly know what I'm about to ask you?"

"Elizabeth told me."

"My sister Elizabeth told you I was about to ask you to marry me?"

"Yes."

"How?"

"She sent a servant girl with a message this morning."

"Why that little —"

"Don't be mad at her, Mr. Roper. It's good I found out this morning. It gave me all day to think about it, and after I'd done some thinking, I realized I don't want to marry you."

"But Miss Dandelion—"

"Mr. Roper, please don't try to change my mind. I'm not the girl for you. That's all there is to it. Now please, I want to be alone now. Go back to the ball and let me be."

Chrissy went to the balcony rail and turned her back on Mr. Roper, but also on *the man*. She felt both pairs of eyes boring in on her. At long last, Mr. Roper went back inside, and there was only *the man*.

He said: "My name is Arthur. Arthur Moore."

She turned to him, surprised at how close he had come to her: "I'm Chrissy Dandelion."

"I know, I wrote you."

"About that," Chrissy said, "please explain this strange feeling I've had today."

"The feeling that you are the main character in a romance novel?"

"Yes, that."

"I wrote that part too, I wanted you to know."

"Explain."

"Take a walk in the garden with me, and I will."

"This will be difficult to explain, Chrissy," said Arthur, "and if I hadn't written you to know much of the truth already, you would never believe it."

The scent of the roses in the garden, combined with the smell of *the man*, overpowered Chrissy. She wanted Arthur to take her in his arms and crush her in his manly embrace. She was hoping that would happen after he had finished explaining what he wanted to explain. She would be patient.

"I'm a writer, and when I'm not writing, I watch television to get inspiration for my writing."

Chrissy was confused.

"What is 'television'".

"A television is a machine, you use it to watch movies."

"I don't understand. What is a 'movie'?"

"A movie is like a play, only you see it through a television."

"I still don't understand."

"Excuse me," Arthur said, smiling. She loved his smile. "Movies and television are things that haven't been invented yet in your world."

"My world?"

"Yes, the fictional world you live in. *This* world."

"There is only one world, Arthur."

"On the contrary, Chrissy, every book ever written describes its own separate fictional world. This world, the one you live in and believe is real, is a world of my creation. Everything in it, everyone in it, including you, is my creation."

Chrissy wasn't sure how to react to what this man was saying. He was either playing a trick on her, was completely delusional, or was telling the truth. The odd idea that had occurred to her at tea time, that she was the main character in a romance novel, was starting to have terrible implications. If this was true, then nothing she'd ever experienced was real.

"Do you have proof that what you say is true?"

"How could I possibly prove such a thing?"

Chrissy pointed at the Moon.

"Make it move."

"The Moon?"

"Yes."

"How would that prove anything if I moved the Moon?"

"You're the writer of this world, aren't you? If that's true, and this is all a product of your imagination, you should be able to do anything. So, prove it and move the Moon."

Arthur closed his eyes and concentrated. Then he opened his eyes:

"I can't."

Chrissy stormed off back to the mansion.

"Where are you going?" He chased after her.

"I'm going to go find Mr. Roper and tell him I will marry him."

"You can't."

"Why not?"

"He's already asked your friend, Violet, to marry him. She said 'yes'."

"How do you know that?"

"Because, Chrissy," said Arthur, "that's the way I wrote it."

Everything got blurry and then the world turned black.

When Chrissy came to, she was in Arthur's arms. They were sitting on a stone bench in the garden, and her head was against his chest.

"What happened?" she asked.

"You fainted."

"Oh my God, how stupid of me. Only ridiculous girls in romance novels faint. I'm so embarrassed."

"There's no need to be embarrassed, no one saw it happen but me."

"Tell me the truth, Arthur. What's happening to me?"

"Let me tell you what inspired me to write this book we're in, and then you'll understand."

"That's a very odd coincidence," Chrissy said. "You watched two movies in two nights, with essentially the same plot?"

"Yes," said Arthur.

"In the first movie, a lonely writer meets his dream girl, but in the end she's only a fictional character he wrote in a book?"

"Yes."

"In the second movie, a lonely writer writes his dream girl as a fictional character, and then she appears in his real life?"

"Yes."

"I think the people making these movies are stealing ideas from each other," she said.

"Yes, that's probably true."

"What happens to these dream girls?"

"In the first movie, when the writer realizes the dream girl is not real, she disappears," said Arthur. "In the second movie, when the dream girl realizes she's not real, she disappears."

"Is that the end?"

"No, at the very end of both movies, another girl who looks exactly like the dream girl shows up and there is a 'happily ever after' ending with the real girl."

"So, seeing these movies inspired you?"

"Yes."

"How?"

"I decided that instead of writing about my dream girl coming into my world, I would go to the dream girl in her world."

"And that's what you're doing now?"

"Yes."

"Am I your dream girl?"

"I hope so."

"You don't know?"

"I've barely met you. The fact is, I didn't write about you in great detail so there's a lot about you I still don't know."

Chrissy had a thought: "Why would you tell me that none of this is real? Doesn't that ruin it?"

"I wanted to be completely honest with you. In the movies I watched, the girl disappears because the truth wasn't known from the beginning, and the realization of the truth breaks the spell. I thought if you knew the truth in the beginning, that wouldn't happen."

Chrissy stood up and put some distance between them. The night air was cooling and she shivered. He went to her, took off his coat and put it around her.

"All of this is too much, Arthur," she said.

"Too much?"

"Take me back to the ball."

"I have so much more to tell you."

"Not now, Arthur. I've got some thinking to do, and I need to be apart from you for a while."

"How long?"

"I don't know — a day, a week, a year? Just take me back to the ball."

CHAPTER THREE

——— ◐ ———

ELIZABETH AND ARTHUR

When Chrissie woke up the next morning there was a girl in bed with her.

The girl was spooning her.

Chrissie was about to go back to sleep, but then realized the girl was naked.

It was Roger Roper's sister, Elizabeth.

Chrissie jumped out of bed and realized — she was naked too.

Empty champagne bottles and glasses told the rest of the story — but Chrissie remembered nothing.

She shook the girl awake.

"What happened? Did we —"

Elizabeth was sleepy but awoke with a start. She looked around the room, her face full of horror.

"Chrissie, I —"

Arthur walked in, saw the two naked girls, and both went diving under the covers.

"Relax, nothing happened last night," he said. "I just had to know, that's all."

"What did you have to know, Mr. Moore?" Chrissie asked him, being stiff and formal despite her nakedness.

"It kind of threw me when I couldn't move the Moon last night," he said. "I had to know what I *could* do."

"What did you do?"

"I'll explain during breakfast," he said. "Your nightgowns are in the closet, in perfect condition since they weren't worn last night."

———————

"Violet told me what you said, Chrissy," said Elizabeth, "that you felt you were the main character in a romance novel. Arthur told me the rest last night."

They were eating breakfast at Arthur's ducal castle, served buffet style on a side table. Chrissy helped herself to a slice of ham, a bit of scrambled eggs, and a glass of orange juice.

"So I'm to be the laughing stock of the county," Chrissy said, sitting next to Arthur, who was seated at the end. Elizabeth had taken the seat next to Arthur on the other side of the table.

"No, Chrissy," said Elizabeth, "I made Violet promise not to tell anyone else, not even Roger."

"What happened last night?" Chrissy asked.

"Nothing that will ruin either of your reputations." said Arthur, "in this world, it never even occurs to people to be suspicious of two girls who share a bed."

"But how did we get here?" Chrissy wanted to know.

"We came here in my carriage, of course," said Arthur. "Don't worry, my servant, Mrs. Walters, served as chaperon. There won't be any talk that you spent the night as my guest."

"Why can't I remember anything?"

"I wrote it that way."

"Oh God, please stop, Arthur."

"I have more to tell you."

"The more you tell me, the less I'm interested in having this 'happily ever after' I thought we'd have before I met you."

"Don't you want the truth?"

"If you insist," said Chrissy, "tell me the truth."

"In my world —" said Arthur.

"The real world," said Elizabeth.

"Yes, in the real world, the year is 2021. I am not, as I appear to you in this world, a young man. I am actually fifty-five years old, divorced, and have three grown children. I do not live in a castle, I live in a three-bedroom house with 1350 square feet. I do not own a horse and carriage, I own a 2017 Toyota Camry —"

"I don't know what that is," said Chrissy.

"It's a type of automobile, they called them 'horseless carriages' when they were first invented."

"A carriage that moves by itself?" Elizabeth asked.

"Yes."

"Oh my God," said Elizabeth, "that's so much better than any carriage drawn by horses."

"But I'm not rich," said Arthur, "that's the point I'm trying to make. Almost everyone in my world has an automobile. Some people have many."

"Do you hear that, Chrissy? In Arthur's world it's everyday to drive about in a carriage that moves by itself."

"Yes," said Chrissy. "I hear it."

"So Arthur," said Elizabeth, "this person who appears to us in this world, is he really you or just an avatar?"

"I would never have expected such a question," Arthur said. He smiled. Elizabeth smiled back.

"I don't understand," said Chrissy. "What's an avatar?"

"It's a Hindu concept," said Elizabeth, "an avatar is the descent in Earthly form of a deity."

"I'm not a deity," said Arthur.

"In this world you are. You created us," said Elizabeth.

"He can't move the Moon," said Chrissy. She took pleasure in saying it.

Elizabeth was astonished.

"You can't move the Moon?" she asked. "How is that possible?"

"My theory is that even though I created this world, it follows the rules I set when I decided what kind of novel to write."

"This world is in a romance novel," said Elizabeth. "The Moon doesn't move about the sky in a romance novel."

"Right," said Arthur, "so even me, the writer, can't move the Moon. I would also guess that I couldn't make things float in the air, or start a fire without matches."

"What if you wrote a fantasy story, where such things are possible?" Elizabeth asked.

"I don't know, Elizabeth," said Arthur. "Perhaps I should try it."

Arthur put down his fork, pushed back his chair, and started walking out of the breakfast room.

"Where are you going?" Chrissy asked.

"To my study," said Arthur, "I'm going to write a fantasy story."

Arthur sat down at his writing desk, grabbed a piece of ducal stationary, and a quill pen. He dipped the pen in an inkpot and put it to the paper.

"How shall I begin?" Arthur asked.

"How about 'Once upon a time,'" Elizabeth suggested. "That's a good start to a fantasy story."

"Once upon a time—"

"How will you put yourself into this story?" Elizabeth asked.

"I'll write a character I like, then concentrate on being him."

"That's all?" Chrissie asked.

"It's not that hard, Chrissie. Every character I write has a piece of me inside."

"Even the women?" Elizabeth wanted to know.

"Yes, even the women. But to make it easier, I'll write a male character."

"Make him a powerful wizard," said Elizabeth. "Then you can move the Moon."

"That's something I'd like to see," said Chrissy.

"Me too," said Elizabeth.

"Why not?" said Arthur. "I'll write in two female characters, and then you two concentrate on being those characters. Then you can be in the story with me."

"Make us wizards too," said Elizabeth.

CHAPTER FOUR

———○———

A NEW WORLD

Chrissie groped around in the dark.

She felt a nose, a cheek, she heard a girl giggling.

"That's me you're touching," said Elizabeth.

Elizabeth touched her back.

"Let there be light," Arthur said.

A light appeared in the sky, and Chrissie could see the three of them, standing alone on a great empty plain. The sky above was dark and empty — no sun, moon or stars — only the light that had just appeared.

"What is this place?" Chrissy asked.

"This is what a world looks like before anything has been created," said Arthur.

"I don't like it here," she said.

"Try creating something," said Arthur.

"You made us wizards, not gods," said Chrissy.

"Try, see what you can do."

"I want the sky to be orange," said Elizabeth.

The sky was orange.

Chrissy had a thought.

"I want this world to look like home," she said.

They were standing in a field of green grass. Arthur's ducal mansion was off in the distance. The full moon was hovering in the sky.

"It doesn't look like home," said Chrissy. "The sky is still orange."

"We are co-creators here," said Arthur. "Elizabeth, try changing the sky."

"Make the sky look like the sky at home," Elizabeth said.

The sky was black and full of thousands of stars, just like home.

"Are we really home?" asked Chrissie. "If we go back to your castle, will we see ourselves there?"

"Do you want to find out?" Arthur asked.

"Yes, and just to be sure of what I want, I want this world to be just as our world was last night when we got home from the ball."

The moon shifted in the sky.

"So, it would appear the Moon can be moved if you say the right words," said Chrissy.

Elizabeth looked like she wanted to say something.

"What?" Chrissy asked.

"Nothing."

——————— ———————

Behind the door to the bedroom, there were noises.

Pleasure noises.

"If I open this door," said Chrissy, "what will I see?"

"Nothing you didn't want to happen," said Elizabeth.

"Who is in there?" Chrissy asked.

Silence.

"Who is in there?"

"The three of us," said Arthur.

"Why don't I remember?"

"Afterwards, you were ashamed," said Arthur. "I rewrote the story so you'd forget."

"I thought we'd have a 'happily ever after', Arthur," said Chrissy, "I thought that was what you wanted."

"I do want a 'happily ever after' with you, Chrissy," said Arthur, "but now it includes Elizabeth."

Elizabeth took Chrissy's hand.

"Chrissy, I've been in love with you since the day we met. I was four and you were six. Do you remember that day?"

"I remember."

"But Roger wanted you too, so I stepped back."

"Yes."

"The reason I agreed to be your spy was I was hoping you would realize Roger wasn't for you. I told you things about him that would make you understand that."

"You made up lies about Roger?"

"No, all of it was true."

"He really screams at the servants?"

"Constantly."

"He really kicked the dog so hard it had to be put down?"

"Yes."

"Why the elaborate ploy, Elizabeth?" said Chrissy, "why not simply tell me the truth?"

The noises in the other room stopped.

"You're about to see, Chrissy, why Elizabeth has never been able to tell you the truth," Arthur said. To the air he said: "We are invisible to the people of this world."

The door opened.

———————————————

The three of them walked into the bedroom and saw themselves. Empty champagne bottles and glasses were scattered around the room. As Arthur had commanded, the people in the room, who were not wearing clothes, did not see their observers.

Chrissy was sitting on the edge of the bed, with Elizabeth's arms around her.

"I can't believe you took advantage of me," Chrissy saw herself saying.

"No one took advantage of anyone," said Elizabeth. "I love you. I've always loved you. And I think, deep down, you've always loved me. That's why this happened. And tonight, since we both are attracted to Arthur, he joined in too."

"No," said Chrissy. "That's disgusting."

"You believe it's disgusting because that's what you've been taught to believe," said Arthur. "There's no more reality to that belief then there is in the tooth fairy."

"Next you'll say there's no God."

"If there is a God," said Elizabeth, "he wouldn't want people to hate themselves because of who they love."

But Chrissy could not be consoled. Finally, she said:

"You're the creator of this world, right Arthur?"

"Yes."

"Then use your power to erase this memory from my mind."

"I don't want to do that."

"If you don't erase this memory, I'll never love you and we will never have a 'happily ever after'."

"Jesus, Chrissy."

"Do it, Arthur," said Elizabeth.

"But—"

"I'll step back, just like I stepped back when Roger wanted her. Two of the three of us will be happy. That's not bad,
when you consider it."

"Elizabeth-"

"Do it. Erase her memory."

They went home, which took just a moment of wanting
to be home. Arthur was back at his writing desk. The two
girls were standing in their nightgowns beside him. It was
morning again, just after breakfast. The minute hand on the
grandfather clock hadn't moved.

"You had second thoughts, didn't you Elizabeth?"
Chrissy asked. "Arthur went to his desk to change the story, but afterwards, you decided to put me in bed naked
and climb in bed naked with me. You didn't clean up the
champagne bottles and glasses. You knew I'd forget, but
you made damn sure I'd still figure out what happened.
Why?"

"I've been wondering that myself," said Arthur.

Elizabeth was in tears.

"I wanted something a woman like me can never have,"
she said. "Even my lesbian friends don't get it. They tell me
I have to choose whether I like men or women. I don't want
to choose, I want both. I thought with the two of you, I
could have it."

The three of them spent the rest of the day in different parts
of the castle, not talking to each other. The servants, sens-
ing the dark mood of their master and his guests, made

themselves invisible. At dinnertime, they barely spoke. But finally, Elizabeth said:

"When you started writing this romance novel, you never thought it would happen like this, did you Arthur?"

"I suppose not, Elizabeth," said Arthur, "we've put a different spin on the love triangle, haven't we?"

"Arthur," said Chrissy, "you've been judging me since last night. Maybe in 2021, where you come from, people are open-minded about who is allowed to love who. But here, in my world, there are rules and a woman in my position can't break them. Even if I wanted a 'happily ever after' in a three-way relationship, that is impossible. My advice to you is to return to your world, and forget about me."

"I will be leaving," said Arthur, "but not to return to my world. From now on, I'll be traveling through worlds of my own creation. I will write fantasy stories, science fiction stories, mystery stories, horror stories, and yes, more romance stories. It will be a grand adventure. Why don't you both come with me? Our love may be impossible here, but I will make sure it's possible in the worlds we visit in the future."

Chrissy took a moment to consider, but only a moment.

"I'm a conventional woman, Arthur, and desire a conventional life. But thank you for your kind offer."

"Elizabeth?"

"Thank you, Arthur, but my place is here with Chrissy. I'm her best friend."

"Very well," said Arthur. He put his fork down and stood up.

"I'm going to my writing table to write myself out of this story. I suggest you both be gone before the real Duke returns to his senses."

"He's not a real Duke," Chrissy said, "he's a fictional character."

"Right, of course."

CHAPTER FIVE

FINISH

The rest of the story can be told quickly.

Chrissy's friend Violet married Roger Roper and at first they were very happy. But it wasn't long before dark rumors circulated through the county that Roger was beating Violet on a somewhat regular basis. The beatings stopped suddenly one day when Violet shot Roger to death with her father's pistol. The police investigated, but every servant who witnessed the shooting swore it was an accident — the gun had misfired while Violet was cleaning it. Roger's will disinherited Violet if she remarried, so she took on the gardener, a man named Charles Doone, as a lover. Violet and Charles lived happily ever after.

Chrissy married the Duke, who turned out to be quite a different sort of man when Arthur was not controlling him as an avatar. He cared nothing at all for sex, but did his duty with Chrissy until she gave birth to a son. After that, he left her alone.

Elizabeth, cut off from her inheritance by her spiteful family, moved in with Chrissy and took a position as her lady's companion. Chrissy and Elizabeth enjoyed many afternoons giving each other pleasure while the Duke puttered around in his study with his stamp collection. Chrissy, Elizabeth, and the Duke lived happily ever after.

Is there a moral to the story? Yes.

If you're a writer, and you meet your dream girl from a story you've written, you must not tell her she's a fictional character you can control by rewriting the story. Telling her that will hurt her feelings, and if she is your lover, it will kill the love she has for you. If you don't believe me, watch the movies *Poor Greg Drowning*, written by Jeffrey Scott Collins, and *Ruby Sparks*, written by Zoe Kazan. I salute these two writers for the inspiration they gave me to write this story.

The End.

BEYOND

THE

STRETCH

CHAPTER ONE

———— ⬤ ————

THE MAP

Aesopicus, our teacher, pointed to the map on the wall. "Who can point to the Inner Kingdoms?" he asked. All of the students, the four of us, raised our hands.

"Hiram," he said to me, "I know you know this, put your hand down." Disappointed, I did.

"Axl," said the old man, "come up here, show us where the Inner Kingdoms are."

Axl, a bit slower than the others, stood up, went to the front and pointed at the map. "Elbrassa, Delva, Manisas, and Regori. The Inner Kingdoms are in the middle of the continent around the coast of the Inner Bay."

"Very good, Axl," said Aesopicus, "You're smarter than people assume because of your bulky size and great strength." The boy beamed happily from the tutor's praise, then went back to his desk and sat down.

"That one was easy," said Anny, the class' only girl and biggest show-off "I'll do a hard one."

Without asking permission, she got out of her desk, went up to the map and said: "These are the Outer Kingdoms,

Vana, Gorin, Kiros, and Nyromi. The Outer Kingdoms are around the Inner Kingdoms, touching the Outer Sea."

"What do we call the Eight Kingdoms as a group? Lars?"

"Calamar," said Lars. He was a pious boy, more interested in learning from the Holy Book than geography. But everyone knew that the Eight Kingdoms were referred to as Calamar.

"Here's one for you Hiram," said our teacher, "where's our village, the village of Palana?"

I stood up to examine the map. Our teacher let me search for a good long time before I said, "It's not here. How can I find our village if it's not here?"

"Yes, indeed, Hiram, Palana is not here," said Aesopicus, "This map was created by a geographer who works for the Emperor of Calamar. If ever the location of Palana is known to the Emperor, our village will be destroyed within a fortnight."

CHAPTER TWO

THE GIRL

"I love you," I said, when I really shouldn't have.

"I am not the girl you will marry," the girl said, whispering in my ear. We were in our usual hiding place, the barn. She lay naked in the straw, with me on top of her.

"I don't care," I said. "I want you."

"I want you too. But it doesn't matter what we want," she said, pushing me off and picking up her clothes. "That's not the way the world works."

"How does the world work?"

"I can't be with you again, Hiram," she said, getting dressed. Then she walked out.

After taking a moment to recover, I got dressed too.

CHAPTER THREE

———— ◐ ————

THE SPELL

"The formula of the spell you're casting is basic to every-thing else we understand about magic," Aesopicus said. "Yet you're failing over and over. You're not concentrating. Is it the girl?"

I had never told him about the girl.

"Yes," I admitted. "She said we can't be together anymore."

"She is correct," said my teacher. "Soon, we will leave this place to rejoin the world outside. She will not be coming with us. She is already in your past. Best to forget about her."

CHAPTER FOUR

———— ● ————

ANNY

I took up with Anny, who was willing enough.

I got too serious: "I love you," I said.

She jumped up and started getting dressed. She was angry.

"What's wrong?"

"You're a fool Hiram, an absolute fool."

"Did I say the wrong thing?"

"We were having fun, then you had to go and ruin it."

"I don't understand."

"I'm not the girl you will marry, either."

CHAPTER FIVE

—— ◖ ——

THE TRUTH

I cornered the old wizard in his laboratory.

"Everyone seems to know something about me that I don't know," I said.

"We kept it from you because we believed it best you not know."

"Maybe you should tell me before someone else does."

"The reason this village is kept secret from the Emperor is you," he said. "He is your uncle, you are a threat to his throne. If he finds out you're still alive, and in this village, he will send soldiers to kill us all."

"Then I should leave."

"Yes, that plan has been in the works since before you were born."

"I should leave now."

CHAPTER SIX

─── ◯ ───

FIRST INTERLUDE

"The story is told by every bard at every campfire in every town in the world," said Princess Genevieve. "And you are the villain every time. And when your nephew arrives to challenge you, he will be the hero."

"My dead brother's faction is rich and powerful, they pay off the bards to tell the tale this way," said the Emperor.

"Taxes are too high."

"To pay for the war with the Caliphate, a war I didn't start and would end if I could."

"Your vassals oppress the people."

"If I cracked down on my lords, they would rebel against me, and the people would be worse off in the civil war that followed."

"You are extravagant in your spending."

"If I wasn't, the people would call me a tightwad, and I'd be even more unpopular."

"You are the Emperor, you can't be as powerless as you claim."

"If your cousin defeats me, and takes the throne, you will marry him and be the Empress. After that happens, you will know the powerlessness of being in power."

CHAPTER SEVEN

—— ● ——

THE CAT

There was something I liked to do when no one was around. A certain stray cat had wandered into the barn two days ago and I had my eyes on him. I cornered him in a stall and kicked him. He howled in pain as his body flew in the air.

I kicked him again.

Then again.

While I was washing my boots, Anny sneaked up behind me.

"Be careful with who you let see you do that, Hiram."

"I am careful."

"If Lars sees you..."

"He won't."

CHAPTER EIGHT

———◉———

I'M PREGNANT

The day came when Aesopicus, Axl, Lars, Anny and I were packed and ready to start our quest through the Eight Kingdoms which would end when we reached the capitol Aasirna to challenge the Emperor, and depose him.

The girl motioned me to come aside.

"I'm pregnant."

"Not my problem."

"You're the father."

"Can you prove it?"

"Listen, I may be just a servant girl, but I don't want to have this baby out of wedlock. It will ruin my chances to get married."

I reached into my purse, pulled out two silver coins, and handed them to her.

"Go to the witch and get an abortion."

Her eyes filled with tears. "I thought you loved me, Hiram."

"You're the one who left me."

She turned to go.

"If you tell anyone about this," I said, "I'll find you and send someone to kill you."

The blood drained out of her face.

"Goodbye," I said. I kissed her forehead. Then she ran away.

We jumped on our horses and left the village.

CHAPTER NINE

———— ◯ ————

TO LAEDELA

"**W**hy don't we take the King's Road straight to the capitol?" I asked.

"This is not an ordinary trip," said Aesopicus. "We are the leading characters in a hero's journey. It is necessary that we take a roundabout route to extend the length of the tale."

"So, where are we going first?"

"To Laedela, land of the elves."

"Elves?" asked Anny. "Maybe they could give me some tips on archery."

"I suppose they could give me pointers on magic," I said.

"They are masters of the sword," said Axl. "I could use a few lessons."

CHAPTER TEN

---○---

THE ELVES

We were surrounded on all sides by elves. None of us had seen them approach through the forest. They had their bows trained on us.

"Watch where you point that thing," I snarled.

"Is it really necessary, Prince Vertisso, that every time elves encounter humans, they ambush us in this way?" Aesopicus asked.

"This tale is already written," said the Prince. "We elves must act as expected so that the truth does not stray from the tale."

"Take us to your village, please, we need to speak to your Queen," the old wizard asked.

"Of course," said the Prince. "That part is also already written."

CHAPTER ELEVEN

———— ◐ ————

THE QUEEN

"**W**e are beset by the Red Moon tribe of orcs," said the Queen, "I cannot spare any warriors to support you in your revolution."

"Then lend us only your best," said the wizard, "an elf who is skillful at sword, bow, and magic, so he can train the young people who travel with us."

"Prince Vertisso," said the Queen, "you will join these humans and accompany them until their quest is completed."

"Yes, your majesty" said the Prince. "I am also a bard, so I can make sure the tale is told correctly."

"Now that that is decided," said the queen, "let us feast!"

The assembled elves cheered.

CHAPTER TWELVE

———— ● ————

THE PARTY

"This is a party, Lars," said Axl the warrior, slurring his words because he'd had too much elf wine to drink, "time to eat, drink, and be merry."

Lars was putting bandages on a pretty elf girl.

"At some point in our adventure we will encounter enemies," said the young cleric, "and I will need to have my healing skills fully trained on that day."

"Very well, Lars, suit yourself." Axl staggered off in the woods to take a piss.

"He didn't notice that except for these bandages, I'm not wearing any clothes," said the elf girl, giggling.

"It's time to take them off now," said Lars. "I can't waste bandages on a test run."

"I'm too drunk to resist you should you remove the bandages and ravish me."

"Milady," said Lars, "if I gave you the impression that I would do such a thing, I extend my deepest apologies."

"Oh, Okay," said the elf girl with a disappointed tone. "I suppose I'm lucky you're such a gentleman."

"Yes, milady," said Lars. "My mother taught me to always be a gentleman with the ladies."

"Your mother had a good heart," said the elf girl.

CHAPTER THIRTEEN

UNWANTED ATTENTION

"Hiram," said Anny, "let go of my arm, you're hurting me."

"Give me what I want," I said, "and I'll stop."

"There's no future in us," said the girl, "you're going to marry the princess."

"What if I don't want to marry the princess?" I said, "what if I want to marry you? I'll be the Emperor, I can marry whoever I please."

"Hiram, please, let me go."

My old teacher called from a distance.

"Anny? Come over here, I have something I wish to discuss with you."

I let go of Anny's arm and she went over to Aesopicus.

"What's the harm in giving him what he wants?" I heard him whisper to her.

"I don't love him," she said.

"He'll be the Emperor," the old tutor said. "Don't piss him off. Now go back to him and give him what he wants."

She returned to me.

"There's a copse of trees over there," she said. "No one will see us."

"I'm all yours," I said.

CHAPTER FOURTEEN

———————◯———————

ELF MAGIC

"The magic you've learned so far has a solid foundation," said the Prince. "But I can teach you elf magic, which taps into the fey world to accomplish things that will surprise your enemy."

"Unless my enemy knows about elf magic," I said.

"Yes, of course, now watch me as I move my hands oh so delicately to entice the fey world to..."

"You entice the fey world? Why don't you command it?"

"You can't give the fey orders, Hiram, that's not how it works."

"When I'm the Emperor, we will see about that."

CHAPTER FIFTEEN

———◗◖———

THE DWARVES

We entered Morth, the dwarf kingdom next. The Dwarf King, Thorin Oakhammer gave us a hearty feast. I sat down next to him at the feasting table.

"I could use your help when I attack the Emperor," I said to him.

"I can spare you three hundred warriors, but you have to promise me something in return."

"What is it?"

"You will throw the Empire's support for me in my war against my rebellious cousin Gallum Oakhammer until I am victorious."

"Consider it done."

Later that evening, Aesopicus approached me.

"You promised to help the King against his cousin?"

"Yes."

"That's unfortunate. The war between the Dwarf King and his cousin has dragged on for three hundred years. Involving the Empire will drain our resources and we are already tied up in a war with the Caliphate."

"Simple to solve, old friend. After the Dwarf King has helped us overthrow my uncle, I will announce that he is lying when he said I'd help him in his war against his cousin, and refuse to send troops. It will be his word against mine, what can he do?"

"Treachery? I suppose you must learn sooner or later that an Emperor must break many of the promises he makes. Just be careful not to betray too many people or it will catch up with you."

"But the tale tells I will be victorious and liberate the people from my uncle."

"Yes, it does. We pay the bards to tell it that way."

"Then pay the bards to leave out the treachery parts and we'll be good."

CHAPTER SIXTEEN

—◉—

ORC ATTACK

Three thousand orcs surrounded us in Mortimer's Pass, in the Belephron Mountains, separating the Outer Kingdoms from the Inner Kingdoms. It was me, my tutor Aesopicus, Prince Vertisso, Lars, Axl, my mistress Anny, and the three hundred dwarf warriors the Dwarf Kingdom sent with us. It was ten to one, but we won easily and we lost only a few score dwarves and no one important to me.

"The orcs knew we were coming this way," I said, "someone betrayed us."

"Not necessarily," said the old wizard, "it's easy to see an army of three hundred approaching."

"We will camp here and interrogate everyone until the spy confesses."

"That will take valuable time," said Aesopicus, "time better spent marching."

"It seems to me you're eager to protect the spy, old friend, perhaps you are the spy."

After nine hours of torture Aesopicus confessed he was the spy, sending secret messages to the Emperor to inform him of our location. No doubt, the Emperor had tipped off the orcs. I ordered my old teacher's body to be hurled in a ditch to be feasted on by vultures.

"We should give him a decent burial," said Lars.

"Question my orders again, and you will join the old man in the ditch."

CHAPTER SEVENTEEN

———————— ● ————————

SECOND INTERLUDE

"**M**y cousin, after defeating an army of orcs you sent to ambush him, has crossed the mountains and is now within the Inner Kingdoms," said the princess. "Perhaps you should go out and meet him, beg for mercy and surrender your throne."

"Not likely," said the Emperor. "I heard what he did to his friend, the wizard. He would have even less mercy on me."

"The wizard died a traitor's death," said the princess. "You will die a tyrant's death."

"Genevieve, if you had to be Empress for five minutes you'd appreciate I'm doing the best I can. The Caliphate is unceasing in it's attacks on our eastern border and I have no choice but to fight them. I must have soldiers, armor and weapons and that's expensive. I have no choice but to keep taxes high to pay for this war I can't get out of. Do you think Hiram will do any better than me?"

"Yes, father, because you betrayed your brother so your reign is under a curse. Hiram is the rightful Emperor, so his reign will be blessed."

"That's superstitious nonsense, Genevieve."

"It's what the bards are singing in every alehouse in the Empire, father, so it must be true."

"I'm going to order that these bards be arrested and thrown into the dungeon."

"That will be even more proof you're a tyrant, father."

"So be it."

CHAPTER EIGHTEEN

———— ● ————

THE COUP

The gates opened when I arrived at the palace. No one would fight to protect the Emperor. He was brought to me in chains.

"Do you have any last words before you die, uncle?"

The Emperor said nothing, but kept his head high in defiance. I used a dehydrating spell to suck the life out of him and he died. I grabbed the crown and put it on my head.

"Where is the princess?"

"I am here," said a young woman who was quite attractive. "I am Princess Genevieve."

"We are to be married," I said, "and live happily ever after. Anny will be my mistress."

"That last part was left out of the bards' tales," griped the princess.

"Let us say that the bards edit the tale so as to avoid confusing people," I said.

CHAPTER NINETEEN

HAPPILY EVER AFTER

"The tale is nearly complete," I said. "With a few addendums. Axl, as my Prime Minister, please tell me what you've accomplished in the past few weeks."

"The war with the Caliphate has ended. We ceded the Kingdom of Nyromi to the Caliph and allowed him to take all the unmarried women as sex slaves."

"Well, it had to be done," I said.

"Your betrayal of the Dwarf King caused him to declare war on the Empire. We threw our support to the rebellious cousin and now he is involved in a two-front war he cannot win. It won't be long before he surrenders and then we'll have him dragged here in chains and executed."

"Sounds good."

"The elves were displeased with our betrayal of the Dwarf Kingdom, so we sent in a troop of rangers to burn down their forest. They fled beyond the Stretch and are unlikely to return."

"Excellent."

"Anny has said she'd rather die than be your mistress, so we have her locked in the tower under suicide watch."

"She'll come around," I said.

"The Empress is pregnant with your child and you will soon have an heir."

"Nice."

"And a woman from your home village has made the journey to see you and she says she has a surprise."

"Did you get her name?"

"She refused to give it to me."

"Let her enter."

A girl came in, holding a baby.

"He's your son, I didn't have the abortion."

"The position of mistress is open, do you want it?"

"Yes."

"Axl, go to Anny's cell and tell her that her services are no longer required. Then chop off her head and bring it to me."

Axl hesitated.

"Are you having a hearing problem, Axl?"

"No, your majesty."

Axl ran off to obey my orders. A few minutes later he walked in with Anny's head in his hands.

"Now we have a happily ever after, right Axl?"

"Of course."

"The moral of the story," I proclaimed, "is that when the bards are singing the tale your way, a happily ever after is guaranteed."

SPACERS

CHAPTER ONE

---◯---

FARM GIRL

My story begins on Omic, a farming world turned dust bowl. Ma and Pa didn't want to sell me to the Spacers, but it was sell me or starve. Ma asked me to forgive them. And to keep in mind I'd be a wife, not a slave.

CHAPTER TWO

---○---

IN THE PEN

They put us Earther girls in a pen, eighty of us, somewhere deep in their starship. We were treated well.

But a prison is a prison. One girl was shot when she tried to take a lifeboat home.

CHAPTER THREE

WEDDING NIGHT

Every year, the Spacer tribes met on a neutral world and had Carnival. Contracts were made, women were exchanged, and there were weddings. I was paired up with a Spacer boy named Ham.

The wedding night was uneventful. I cried bitter tears, missing Ma and Pa, and Ham didn't try to touch me.

In the morning he slipped into bed beside me. Despite my unhappiness, I responded to him.

CHAPTER FOUR

—◯—

CHILDBIRTH

I gave birth, but they took away the baby.

"It is the Way," said my husband-sister Rhea.

"The Way is harsh," said the mid-wife, "but necessary. You would not want to mother such a child."

"At least let me see her," I said.

"She is already gone," said the mid-wife.

CHAPTER FIVE

———◐———

THE CONTRACT

"**A**re we pirates or protectors?" I asked Rhea, after the battle.

"It depends on who's holding the contract," she said. "We are pirates in the morning. Anti-pirates in the afternoon."

"No wonder the Earthers hate us."

"The Earthers hate us because we're free," said Rhea, "while they are tied to the ground."

CHAPTER SIX

———— ● ————

IT IS THE WAY

Ham died in the next battle. I was a widow and free to re-marry. This time, I would get a choice.

I chose Jem, an Earther man who had joined the Spacers to avoid a debt at home.

"Why me?" he asked on our wedding night.

"The radiation of space spoils the seed of the Spacer men," I said. "With you, I might have a healthy child."

My gamble paid off. I had a child, and this time, the midwife let me keep her.

"'Eastern Star' will be your true name," I told my daughter during the Naming. "But you shall be called 'Ester.'"

"An auspicious name," said Rhea.

But Jem was a worthless man who kept falling into more debt. In orbit over Osteri, I divorced him and ordered he be spaced.

"It is the Way," said Rhea. "A starship is not big enough to hold a woman and her ex-husband."

CHAPTER SEVEN

ESTER

Ester grew into a strong young woman. She killed the Captain and took command of the ship.

"The Spacers would be strong if we united under one leader, and took control of the Gates."

"That is not the Way," said Rhea.

"The Way can change," said Ester.

CHAPTER EIGHT

———— ● ————

COUP

Ester made her move during Carnival. She ordered her men to attack the tent where the Mothers were meeting, and kill every one.

"I am the Grand Mother," she said, "under me, the Spacers will be one people."

"That is not the Way," said an old man. Ester ordered her husband, Kiam, to kill the old man. He struck off his head and hurled it into the crowd. The Spacers bowed in submission.

"We take the Gates," Ester ordered.

CHAPTER NINE

WAR

Taking the Gates was easy, but now the Empire was against us. The war lasted a decade, but our people prevailed.

"I am the Empress," Ester said to me during the victory parade. "And you are the Empress' mother. I grant you anything you desire."

"I desire an end to the killing," I said.

"That is the one thing I cannot grant you."

"Then return me to Omic, my original home."

CHAPTER TEN

FARM WOMAN

Omic was recovered from the drought. Ma and Pa prospered and welcomed me home. I put away my finery and became a farm woman.

ANNIE

THE

SEX ROBOT

CHAPTER ONE

―――――――― ● ――――――――

INITIALIZE PROGRAM

I came online on August 31, which was a Wednesday, leaving just enough time for the factory to finish my programming and send me to a brothel for Labor Day weekend.

I am Annie the Sex Robot, and this is my story.

The first test, as it is for any Sex Robot, was whether I could achieve an orgasm.

A mechanical probe was used, and I passed the test with flying colors.

The second test was whether I could achieve orgasm with a human male.

I passed this test too.

Finally, they paired me with a female human and for some reason, my orgasm was more pleasurable to me than with the male.

The engineers opened the panel in my back, fiddled with my knobs and dials and fixed me. The owners of the factory did not want word getting out to their mostly male customers that their female-equipped Sex Robots preferred women over men.

They paired me with new partners, and this time my pleasure levels were within acceptable limits. I was packed in a box and shipped to a brothel.

CHAPTER TWO

TRIX

When I woke up I was in a small room, lit only by a red neon light. I was sitting on a piece of furniture that would serve the function of bed, though it was hard like a bench, and had no pillows or sheets. I would lay there on my back while humans had sex with me. Or, I would have sex with humans in 511 other positions.

The door opened and my first customer walked in. It was a human female, and I wished at that moment they had not taken away the extra pleasure I got from having sex with females.

She was young, and wanted to talk to me first. I was programmed to oblige.

"Hello," she said, "I'm Trix. What's your name?"

"I'm Annie," I said. I could say a lot more, but I was programmed to let the human take the lead.

"Annie, is it OK if I touch you here?"

Trix reached out and touched my breast. I wondered why she had asked permission. I wondered why she had touched me before I gave permission. I wondered why she hadn't figured out yet that I was a Sex Robot and she could do whatever the hell she wanted to do to me.

But I let all these questions stay in my robot brain, unspoken. I said:

"Yes Trix, you may touch me there if you please."

The girl kept her hand on my breast for a few moments, then moved her hand to my other breast. It was a mildly pleasurable experience for me.

"You wanna' hear something funny my boyfriend said?" Trix asked me.

Trix had paid for fifteen minutes with me, so there wasn't time for funny stories. But I said:

"Sure."

"My boyfriend said my name 'Trix' would be a good name for a Sex Robot. What do you think? Isn't that funny?"

She was asking me for my opinion on a joke. I didn't understand the joke, so I faked it:

I let out a girlish peal of laughter.

The girl laughed with me, and this gave her the notion that she should touch me down below. I spread my legs apart to give her better access. As I was programmed to, I experienced pleasure.

When it was over, the human girl Trix pulled up her bluejeans shorts and zipped them closed. Then she put on her shirt. I had no clothes to put on, which caused her to say:

"They make you sit there naked all night? That's not right."

The girl was coming close to the end of her fifteen minutes. I wanted her to leave.

"I don't mind," I said.

"But you *should* mind," she said. "Even a Sex Robot should be treated with some minimal amount of respect."

She had paid the brothel to have sex with me. Now she wanted to be my savior.

"Your boyfriend is waiting outside for you, isn't he?" I asked. "He must be eager to see you."

"I'm going to go talk to the people who run this joint," she said. "I'm not leaving until they give you a decent set of clothes."

Maybe she'd forgotten I was a Sex Robot. I looked so human it was easy to forget. To make us better sex partners, Sex Robots could do almost anything a human could do. We ate human food, which we removed in a plastic sack after the meal. We simulated breathing, even while in rest mode. We even sweat when we're hot, or during the throes of passion.

My programmers knew this could happen, a human deciding she wanted to rescue me. My program for this eventuality kicked in. I said:

"Please don't cause a scene, Trix. If you demand they give me clothes, they will. But once you're gone, they'll take the clothes away and beat me as punishment for embarrassing them."

Her big brown eyes grew bigger:

"They wouldn't dare!"

"They would," I insisted. "Please leave and forget you ever met me."

"I'm sorry," said the girl. "But there's no way I'm just going to leave you here now that I know how horrible these people are."

CHAPTER THREE

—— ● ——

NEW FRIEND

Trix bought me and took me home. Her father barely looked over his newspaper when I walked in the front door. Her mother said: "Does your friend want a snack? I just made a batch of cookies."

Like I said, I was made to look human.

"Come upstairs to my room, Annie," said the girl.

As programmed to, I obeyed.

———————

Trix' room had two beds.

"I share this room with my sister, but she's away at college so you can sleep in her bed," Trix explained to me.

I lay down in the bed Trix indicated, and cycled into rest mode.

Trix shook me awake.

"I didn't mean sleep now, Annie. We'll sleep later. Right now, I want to go over some ground rules."

I sat up and paid attention to my owner.

"If Mom and Dad find out you're a Sex Robot, they'll make me take you back. So, we're not going to tell them."

"You want me to lie?" I asked.

"No, Annie, I don't want you to lie. But there's a difference between lying and keeping a secret."

"You want me to keep it a secret that I'm a Sex Robot?"

"Yes."

"OK."

"In fact, don't tell anyone you're a Sex Robot, especially my brother, Harry. If he finds out, he'll tell everyone and I'll be humiliated."

"OK."

"And another thing, Mom and Dad don't know I'm bi, so don't tell them that either."

"OK."

There was a knock on the door.

"That's my boyfriend, Robbie. Open the door and let him in."

———

Robbie came in and closed the door. He was tall, handsome, and had long blond hair. I felt pleasure just looking at him. He looked me up and down and let out a long whistle.

"You went through with it and bought the Sex Robot, Trix? I told you not to. Now, your Mom and Dad will figure out I took you to a brothel and they'll kill me."

"They won't figure out anything because we're going to tell everyone she's human."

Robbie's expression went dark: "You're insane, Trix. You'll never pull that off."

"She's designed to look human, Robbie. Tell the truth, would you know she's a Sex Robot just by looking at her?"

"I'll admit she looks human, but I'm guessing she doesn't act human. She's programmed for brothel work. If she's put in any other situation, she'll flub it."

"Like what?"

"School."

"Why should I take her to school?"

"Because, Trix, if you don't your parents will wonder why she doesn't go to school. You're going to have to come up with some story why she's living here, and not with her parents, and you'll have to take her to school."

CHAPTER FOUR

───────● ●───────

EXCHANGE STUDENT

Trix took me to St. Clara's High School. The teacher, Mrs. Peters, made me stand in the front of the class, while the other boys and girls sat down:

"This is Annie Smith," she said, "an exchange student from Canada. Annie will be attending our school this year. Please make her feel welcome."

The boys and girls looked at me.

"Welcome to our school, Annie," Mrs. Peters said in a high-pitched chirpy voice.

"Welcome to our school, Annie," the boys and girls said, but lacking enthusiasm.

The class was American Literature. The first book we discussed was Mark Twain's *Adventures of Huckleberry Finn*. Trix had given me a data chip to read.

"Who wants to tell the class his or her thoughts about *Huckleberry Finn*?" the teacher asked.

I was ready. I raised my hand.

"Annie?"

I stood up: "The book was a pleasure to read," I said. Then I sat down.

Mrs. Peters looked at me:

"Do you care to elaborate?"

"No."

"Elaborate anyway. What was the book about?"

"The book was about a boy named Huckleberry Finn riding down the Mississippi River on a raft with his friend Jim."

"What was the book *really* about?"

"I don't understand your question."

"Was the book about the injustice of slavery in the antebellum South?"

"No, it was not."

"Then what was the book about?"

"The book was about a boy named Huckleberry Finn riding down the Mississippi River on a raft with his friend Jim."

The next class was Algebra.

"Who volunteers to solve this equation: X squared equals four?" Mr. Roberts asked.

"I volunteer," I said. "X equals two."

"That's good, Miss Smith. Can you tell us how you solved the equation?"

"I have a logic chip in my brain that performs mathematical functions."

"Excuse me?"

Trix leaned forward and whispered to me.

"I'm having my period," I said. "May I be excused?"

Mr. Roberts made a face:

"Next time, Miss Smith, just ask to be excused. I don't need the details."

"May I be excused too?" Trix asked.

"Of course."

In the girl's room I said: "I didn't like lying to him about having a period."

"But now, he's convinced you're a human girl," said Trix. "He was so disgusted he will forget what you said about having a chip in your brain."

———————◆◆———————

Trix, Robbie and I met in the cafeteria and had lunch. I took bites out of a bologna sandwich, which would go in my food sack. Harry, Trix' older brother, joined us. He had dark, wavy hair, eyes the color of the sky after a spring shower has washed it clean, a firm, manly jaw, well-toned muscles in his chest and arms. A human girl might have fallen in love with him. I felt — pleasure.

He looked at me.

"What part of Canada are you from, Annie?" he asked.

"Vancouver," I said, as Trix and I had agreed. I had all the data on the city and was eager to share it: "Vancouver is located in the province of British Columbia, has a population of 631,486 and an area of 338 square miles..."

"Harry doesn't need all the details, Annie," Trix interrupted.

In obedience to my owner, I stopped talking.

"Annie, don't listen to Trix. She's just being rude," said Harry. "Tell me more about Vancouver."

"I can't."

"Why not?"

My instructions were to keep it a secret from Harry that I was a Sex Robot. So, I couldn't tell him that Trix was my owner who I had to obey.

"I can't tell you why not."

"Why can't you tell me why not?"

"I can't tell you that either."

"Wait, back up. What exactly is it you can't tell me?"

"I can't tell you more about Vancouver," I said. "I can't tell you why I can't tell you more about Vancouver. I can't tell you why I can't tell you why I can't tell you more about Vancouver...."

"She's gone into a recursive loop," observed Robbie. "Tell her to stop talking."

"Stop talking, Annie," said Trix.

I stopped talking.

Harry looked at me, looked at Trix, looked at Robbie, then looked at me again. He frowned.

"What the hell is going on?"

CHAPTER FIVE

—— ● ——

HARRY

The way Harry looked at me when he thought I was a human girl gave me pleasure. That pleasure went away when he found out I was a Sex Robot. I couldn't feel sad, but the loss of the pleasure Harry gave me made me lose pleasure in other things. I resolved to get the pleasure back, and to do that I would make Harry fall in love with me. I found him under a tree, looking at the stars. I sat down in the grass next to him.

"That constellation is the Big Dipper," he said, pointing at the sky. "Follow that side of the bowl, and it leads to the North Star."

"I love you, Harry," I said. It wasn't true, of course. But it made sense to me to say it.

"Annie, you're a Sex Robot. You're not programmed for love, you're programmed for pleasure."

"If you loved me, I would feel pleasure. So, what's the difference?"

—— ● ——

Harry took me to the Homecoming Dance. It felt pleasurable to wear a nice dress and to dance with the boy I would love if I was programmed for love.

"Kiss me," I said.

"Would it give you pleasure if I did?"

"Yes."

"But that's all it would give you."

"None of the others care about that, why should you?"

"The others? Who?"

"Trix, Robbie, a few of Robbie's friends."

"They have sex with you?"

"Of course."

Harry's face turned red, and he stormed off.

"Why was he angry?" I asked Trix after the dance.

"You made him jealous," said Trix.

"But I'm a Sex Robot, what does he expect?"

"I don't know, Annie."

The day after Thanksgiving, Harry took me to a seafood restaurant. He ordered salmon. I ordered trout.

"We can have sex anytime you want," I said.

"I don't want that from you."

"What do you want?"

"I want you to love me."

"Funny, that's what I want from you."

We had sex that night. He took it slow, was gentle, and kind. I experienced such pleasure I never knew possible. I felt safe, loved. I wished mightily I could love him back. But I was a Sex Robot, and love was not in my programming.

There was only one way I could stop him from hurting inside. I had to break it off with him.

"I know," he said.

"You know what?"

"I know what you're going to say."

"We can't be together Harry, it hurts you too much."

"I know."

"If there was any way..."

"There isn't."

CHAPTER SIX

———— ● ————

BROTHEL

Trix sold me back to the brothel.

"She's used now," said the owner. "I can only give you half what you paid for her."

"That will do."

The owner transferred the funds to Trix' credit chip.

"Please, promise me you won't beat her," Trix said.

"Why the hell would I do that?"

"She said..."

"Sex Robots are trained to lie to customers in certain situations. Is that why you bought her, because she said I would beat her?"

Trix looked angry:

"Yes."

The owner had a good laugh:

"This unit is very expensive, as you know since you paid full price for her. I would no more beat her then I'd beat a luxury sports car or a fine set of tools."

Trix stood up and turned to leave.

"I'm sorry," I said to her back as she walked out of the office. She didn't say goodbye. She wouldn't even look at me.

I had lost Harry. Now I'd lost Trix too.

———————

It was Christmas Day.

"I'm putting you back to work, Annie," said the brothel owner. "And to make up for the life of ease you've had for the last few months, I'm putting you on double shifts."

After that, men came streaming into my room. None of them were gentle and kind like Harry had been. Some of them got rough, and the brothel owner had to do some repairs. I got no pleasure in any of it. My face got hard, and I got all cold inside. But the men kept coming and coming and coming and coming.

By New Year's Eve, there wasn't much left of me.

The brothel owner could see I was of no more use to him, and he tossed me into a recycle bin.

CHAPTER SEVEN

—◯—

MRS. JOHNSON

Harry came back for me, but the driver of the recycling truck got there first.

"You can't take stuff out of the bin, kid," said the man. "Once it goes in the bin it's the property of Recycling Services Enterprises, Inc."

"She's mine," said Harry, "I love her."

I knew it was true, but he had never said it. Hearing him say it now made my circuits warm up.

"Take it up with Corporate," said the driver.

"I'll pay you. How much do you want?"

"I can't sell company property. I'd lose my job."

I heard a strange noise coming from Harry. I couldn't see him because I was covered with plastic soda bottles.

"Kid, what's the matter?" said the driver. "Are you crying? For Christ's sake, are you crying?"

"No."

He was.

There was a long pause while the driver thought things over.

"OK kid, here's what we'll do. Grab the robot out of there and put her in the passenger seat of the truck. You sit next to her and the three of us will go to Corporate. We'll sort this thing out. Just stop crying, OK kid? I'm starting to cry too and it's getting embarrassing."

———

They put me in the truck and Harry held me all the way downtown to Corporate. It was an office on the 81st floor of a skyscraper. Harry carried me through the rotating doors into the lobby, into the elevator, and through a vast maze of cubicles and suites into the manager's office. The driver introduced Harry to a woman named Mrs. Johnson, and we all sat down. I was not feeling good, and Harry had to hold me to keep me from slumping to the floor.

"She's pretty banged up, Harry," said Mrs. Johnson. "Wouldn't you be happier with a new one? I have some re-furbished models in my shop. I can give you a good price."

"This is the one I want," said Harry.

"She's worth more for spare parts in her present condition."

"Please, ma'am, sell her to me. I don't care about her condition."

"He's formed an attachment to her," said the driver, try-ing to be helpful.

Mrs. Johnson steepled her hands on her desk and looked serious.

"I've heard of such things," said Mrs. Johnson. "Harry, listen to me. Sometimes a human gets feelings towards a Sex Robot..."

"Please don't call her that."

"But Harry, these feelings of love can never be returned. She's a machine, incapable of love. She is programmed to feel pleasure, and may feel pleasure in your presence. This may feel like love, but it is not."

"I *do* love him," I said.

"Robots are known to lie about such things," said Mrs. Johnson.

I *had* lied about loving Harry, but this time, I meant it. Something had changed inside of me.

"How can I prove I love him?" I said.

Mrs. Johnson had the answer in an instant:

"You can prove you love this boy by letting him go."

———————— ▪ ▬————————

My answer was just as quick:

"No," I said. "I won't let Harry go. I love him and he loves me."

"Think about what's in the boy's best interests," said Mrs. Johnson. "Should he go on, hopelessly in love with a machine? Or do you let him go, so he can make room in his heart for a human girl? A girl who will grow into a woman while he grows into a man. Don't you see, Annie? Marriage, children, growing old together. You can't give him any of that. All you can do is get in the way."

I hesitated.

"You know I'm right," said Mrs. Johnson.

"I know you're right," I said.

I stood up:

"Show me the way to the recycling plant. I wish to be taken offline and destroyed as soon as possible."

Harry howled with grief, fell on his knees and clung to me. I stroked his head with gentleness. The feeling of his hair flowing through my fingers gave me a feeling of pleasure beyond my capacity to measure or describe:

"There, there, Harry. There, there."

———————————

Mrs. Johnson was a tough businesswoman, but she was also a mother with two teenage boys of her own. She said:

"Harry, I won't recycle Annie. I won't sell her to a brothel. She will be re-programmed for office work and I'll put her to work on this floor as a secretary."

She gave Harry a hug. He cried on her shoulder. It took an hour before he was ready to leave.

"Good bye, Harry," I said, extending my hand to shake his.

"Good bye, Annie," he said.

With a last look, he turned to go. The driver left with him to show him the way back to the lobby.

"Thank you for lying to him," I said to Mrs. Johnson. "He'll sleep easier believing I'm being taken care of. Which way is it to the recycling plant?"

"I wasn't lying," said Mrs. Johnson. "I'm sending you to the shop to get you fixed up. Monday morning you're to report to this office to be my secretary."

"But I'm a Sex Robot."

"You *were* a Sex Robot," said Mrs. Johnson. "But only I and the driver know that. We will let a few of the engineers know so they can maintain you, but except for them, everyone in this office will believe you are human."

"I don't understand."

"Understand this, Annie. You have learned what it is to love, and be loved, and in this way you've become more human than some who claim to be human ever will be — including that brothel owner. I won't take that away from you. You will work here as an employee, not a slave. You will be paid a fair wage, enough for you to get an apartment, a car, and whatever else you need. I will use my contacts to obtain identification for you so that if anyone questions that you are human, you will have proof that you are. Do you have any questions?"

"What do I do until Monday?"

"Use the weekend to buy clothes and find an apartment. Here's a credit chip and a key card to my penthouse. You can stay with me until you have your own place."

"I don't know what to say."

"This would be the appropriate time to say:'Thank you, Mrs. Johnson.'"

"Thank you, Mrs. Johnson."

EPILOGUE

That was five years ago, and since then I've lived the life of a human woman in a human-dominated world. Every six months, I have the engineers work on my face to make me appear older. As a single woman, I've made friends with other single women. On weekend nights my friends and I out to bars and nightclubs. I've dated a few men, but I've never reached the point in a relationship where it's serious enough I'd have to reveal I'm not really human.

One summer day, I took the afternoon off and drove over to Harry and Trix' house to spy on them. They were swimming in the pool in the backyard, and both of them appeared to be quite happy. I'm glad.

Will I ever love another man the way I loved Harry?

That's a question I'll ask myself until the day I go offline, or until the day I meet that man, whichever comes first.

AN
ORDINARY
MAN

FORWARD BY THE AUTHOR

I am reluctant to tell the tale, and yet must.

When you hear it, it will up-end your way of looking at the world.

Things you believed to be true, you will come to learn are not true.

Things you assumed were not true, you will believe.

You will wish you could return to not knowing, but the journey back to not knowing will be impossible for you.

With that warning given, you can stop reading now.

Or you can proceed, sacrificing happy ignorance for un-happy knowledge.

Your choice.

CHAPTER ONE

—— ◉ ——

GOSPIN

Gospin was an ordinary man. And in saying he was ordinary, I am not saying he was ordinary in every way.

He was quite rich. He was the eldest son of a duke, and when his father died he became duke in his father's place. This happened when he was three years old, so he had no memory of not being the duke. He was raised by his mother and by his maternal grandfather, they shared the castle with him. He was their lord, but until he reached the age of majority, he was expected to obey them and he did.

Gospin, being ordinary, never questioned his place in the world. Most of the people around him were servants and they made sure he was fed, bathed, clothed and never allowed to grow bored or unhappy. His mother had many duties around the castle, but she spent enough time with Gospin so he wouldn't feel unloved. They brought children to him, or brought him to the homes of other children, so he would have playmates his age.

His tutor, a man named Spencer, was hired when he was six years old and from that age on, Gospin was educated in mathematics, literature, Greek, Latin, the sciences and the arts. Gospin had a telescope with which to observe the heavens, and a microscope to observe the world of the smallest creatures. He took to reading the classics and the King James version of the Bible.

Gospin went to church on Sunday and it never occurred to him to question the existence of God or the Church of England's version of Christianity. When he was of age, he attended balls and parties, and began a relationship with one young lady that resulted in a proposal of marriage. Both families were delighted with the match, and negotiations were entered concerning the dowry and other such matters. A Christmas wedding was planned.

One summer afternoon, Gospin took a walk on his back lawn and contemplated his life. He was content, it had never occurred to him not to be. Now that he had a match with a good woman, it seemed he would live well for the rest of his days. Gospin had the good sense to be happy when there was no reason not to be.

So, it was all very surprising to Gospin when a saucer-shaped object soared down from the sky and landed on his lawn thirty feet in front of him. He was even more surprised when tiny little creatures came out of the saucer, aimed a weapon at him and stunned him with a ray of light. The surprise turned to shock and indignation when the creatures grabbed him and pulled him into their ship.

Gospin had been kidnapped by aliens, ending the ordinariness of his life.

CHAPTER TWO

―――――● ●―――――

LITTLE GREEN MEN

"**W**here am I?" Gospin asked the little green men who had kidnapped him.

"It would be more appropriate to ask 'When am I?'" said the Leader. Gospin knew he was the Leader without being told.

"Why should I ask 'When am I?'" Gospin asked.

"You humans will have a scientist named Einstein, one hundred years after your time, who will posit as unbreakable law that it is impossible to travel through space faster than the speed of light."

The Leader stopped speaking. Gospin realized he was supposed to say something in return. He said: "And?"

"We Gvorkians break Einstein's law by traveling backwards in time, making it possible to travel through space as fast as we please."

"I see," said Gospin, "then let me ask the question you wish me to ask: 'When am I?'"

"Unfortunately, the answer would make no sense to an Earthling," said the Leader, "let us only say that as we speak your planet is still cooling off from the powerful forces unleashed at the birth of your universe and does not yet have even the smallest speck of life. On the other hand, the surface of your planet was rendered lifeless when your star died billions of years ago."

"Both could not be true."

"But both are true, Gospin. It's a paradox, but there you have it."

"Why am I here?"

"That is an excellent question, Gospin. Had you not asked it we would have insisted on telling you anyway."

"Well, I suppose it's an obvious kind of question."

"You are here because you have been chosen. We have important knowledge to convey to you, which we wish you to spread to your fellow Earthings. You are a wealthy man with much influence in your society, and therefore, have the resources to spread this knowledge to your entire world."

"What is this knowledge you wish me to spread to my people?"

"There is no God."

Gospin was astonished.

"That's it? There is no God?"

"Yes, that's the knowledge we wish you to spread to your fellow Earthlings. Now hold on a few seconds. We will put you back where and when we found you. After that, you can spend the rest of your life spreading the important knowledge that there is no God."

"Excuse me, for just a moment?"

"What is it?"

"Do you have proof there is no God?"

"Proof?"

"Yes, I'm afraid I need proof. If you want me to devote my life to telling people there is no God, I'm going to need some proof."

"I'm sorry, but is it a matter of money? We chose you, Gospin, because you already have money. We didn't expect you to ask for money."

"It's not about money. It's just that what you're asking me to tell people will be quite disturbing to them and if I'm going to convince people there is no God I need proof."

The Leader spoke a few words to his shipmates in his alien language. They started making noises that sounded suspiciously like giggles. Finally, the Leader said:

"Gospin, really, you greatly amuse us. Don't you see that the burden of proof is on you, the theist, to prove there *is* a God? I, the one who posits that there is no such thing as God, have a much more reasonable position, and therefore I don't have to prove anything. It's an application of Occam's Razor, don't you see? Now be a good fellow and go tell the people of your world there is no God."

Gospin was an ordinary man, that part I've already told you, but even he could see there was a problem with the alien creature's argument. Unfortunately, he lacked the capacity to figure out exactly what it was. Therefore, he fell back on something his mother had taught him to rely on when all else fails — common sense. Even a horse has common sense. No matter how much you spur a horse forward, it will not knowingly walk off a cliff to its death.

"If there is no God," Gospin asked, "how is that you and me are here debating whether God exists? How did the universe come to be? How can there be a watch without a watchmaker?"

"I'm not going down that rabbit hole with you, Gospin."

"Tell him the proof," said another creature.

"It's forbidden. Order One."

"As Chief Metaphysics Officer, I override Order One. Tell him."

"Telling him may destroy his effectiveness as a spokes-man to his people."

"Tell him."

The Leader thought it over.

"Gospin, our people have discovered proof there is no God, but I beg you not to force me to tell it."

"If you don't tell me your proof, I will refuse to spread your message."

"Very well, here it is —"

FIRST INTERLUDE

———— ◑ ————

PROOF

This is the proof that the Leader of the Gvorkians told Gospin that there is no God:

EDITOR'S NOTE: FOR THE SAFETY OF OUR READERS, WE HAVE DELETED THIS PORTION OF THE STORY.

Pretty convincing, right?

CHAPTER THREE

———— ● ————

ANNE

They let Gospin off on the back lawn of his estate, at the exact same place and at the exact same moment in time they had picked him up.

"I don't feel right about leaving him here," said the Leader. "He doesn't look well."

"He knows the truth," said the Chief Metaphysics Officer. "Feel good about the fact that this Earthling knows the truth. It is up to him to figure out how to deal with it."

"But why is to so important to Command to tell the Earthlings this truth. Gospin was happy with his theism. Now he is unhappy."

"Knowing the truth is more important than happiness," said the Chief Metaphysics Officer.

The two creatures got back in their spaceship and it hurled into the sky.

Three hours later, Gospin's fiance, Lady Anne, found him, staring into the sky. She looked up into the heavens, trying to discern what he was looking at.

"We've been looking for you, darling. It's getting cold and you'll catch a chill. Please come in."

"What would you say, Anne, if I told you there is proof that God doesn't exist. That everything we were taught in Sunday school is a lie. Jesus didn't die to redeem us. He didn't rise from the dead. There is no heaven or hell. When we die, we stop existing."

Anne grabbed Gospin's hand.

"Is there such proof, dear?"

"Yes, and I know what it is."

Anne thought about this for a long, long time.

"Then I ask you as a mercy to keep it to yourself."

CHAPTER FOUR

———— ● ————

SO WHAT?

Gospin recovered his wits over the next week, gradually processing the fact that there is no God.

Some men find it easy to live with this knowledge, but for Gospin it was nearly unbearable. He had always been happy, and people had assumed his happiness was the natural result of the privileged life he lived — his vast wealth, the company of friends and family — he had never been lonely, or hungry, or wanted for anything. But none of that turned out to be the root of Gospin's happiness. The reason Gospin had been happy was because he believed in a God who loved him, a God who watched over him, a God he would meet after death and be with forever.

The alien creatures had taken his faith from him, leaving him empty and hollow. He was a young man, and questioned whether the rest of his life, getting married, having children, getting older, was worth it when all that awaited him after death was nothingness.

Anne talked to Gospin, tried to ease his suffering, but what could she do? Her fiance was inconsolable. She consulted with the pastor at the local parish, who loaned her books containing all the most convincing arguments for theism from the greatest theist philosophers and theologians. Because Gospin was a man of great wealth, he could afford to consult with these men personally, and at his expense, they traveled to his estate to meet with him. None of it availed, because Gospin had heard the Gvorkian's proof there is no God, and he could not erase it from his mind.

Finally came the day when Gospin was in his study, a pistol in his hand, with half a mind to end his life. Anne found him there, and instead of taking the gun out of his hand, she talked to him.

"Let us say I agree with you, dear, that there is no God. So what?"

"I can't put it in words, Anne. I can't tell you why I feel the way I do. I just don't see a reason to keep on living."

"How about me, Gospin? How about my love for you? Isn't my love for you big enough to sustain you even if there is no God?"

"The feelings of love you have for me are nothing more than the stimulation of nerves caused by chemicals flowing through your body. Your love is the product of a biological instinct so that the human species reproduces. You love me for the same reason a monkey desires to eat a banana. Instinct, survival, evolution. There is no such thing as love."

Anne had finally had enough. She drew back her hand and with all her strength slapped Gospin. He was momentarily startled and the pistol dropped out of his hand.

Thank God, the pistol did not fire a shot when it hit the floor. The trajectory of the bullet would have struck Gospin's heart, killing him instantly.

"Enough!" Anne shouted.

"Enough?"

"Yes, enough! According to you, I am nothing more than an animal with a nervous system, stimulated by chemicals that cause me to think I love you. But how could I love you? I have no mind to love you with. All there is to me is a mass of gray matter called the brain, but this brain doesn't think, it just thinks it can think. There is nothing more to me than molecules, linked together by biological processes. You started by saying God doesn't exist. Don't you see, that if God doesn't exist, I don't exist either? You do not have before you a woman who loves you. All you have is a blob of tissue, bones, and water."

"Anne, I didn't mean —"

"You didn't?"

"Anne, I'm sorry I said there is no such thing as love. That was cruel."

"But that's where you end up, Gospin, when you say there is no God."

"Anne, you've almost convinced me, but I haven't told you the proof there is no God. It's undeniable."

"Where did you hear this proof?"

"Don't laugh."

"Gospin, dear, I am far beyond the capacity to laugh. If I don't rescue you from this dark spell, I may never laugh again."

"Creatures from another world gave me the proof there is no God."

It did not occur to her to doubt him. "Let's hear it," she said.

"No, Anne. I couldn't."

"Tell me, Gospin."

Gospin told Anne the proof there is no God.

It took a while, but Anne processed it. But then, she tossed it out of her mind as useless to her.

"Let me counter that with this argument —"

SECOND INTERLUDE

—— ◐ ——

COUNTERPROOF

This is the proof that Anne gave her fiance Gospin that there MUST be a God:

EDITOR'S NOTE: THE ROYAL SOCIETY OF ATHEISTS AND FREETHINKERS HAVE URGED THAT IF WE DO NOT INCLUDE THE GVORKIANS' PROOF THERE IS NO GOD IN THIS STORY, AS A MATTER OF FAIRNESS, WE SHOULD NOT INCLUDE LADY ANNE'S PROOF THERE MUST BE A GOD. WE AGREE.

CHAPTER FIVE

---○---

LOVE

"How about it, Gospin. Do you think you can go back to living your life, not knowing for certain whether God exists, but having faith that he does, and the hope of heaven that comes with having that faith?"

"Yes, I think I can."

"And most importantly, Gospin, can you love me and accept my love, knowing our love for each other would not be possible if there is no God?"

"Yes, I think I can."

"And Gospin, here's what I propose. You start loving everyone. Instead of moping about your castle, wondering if there is or isn't a God, start loving everyone. God has blessed you with far more wealth than you could possibly need in a lifetime. I propose that for the rest of your life, you use that wealth to donate generously to charities that feed the hungry, clothe the naked, cure the sick, and give shelter to those who lack a roof over their head. If you do that, you will soon forget this so-called proof that there is no God."

EPILOGUE

EXTRAORDINARY

Gospin and Lady Anne were married on Christmas Day and for the rest of their lives they were very happy.

Gospin was no longer an ordinary man. He was extraordinary.

ABOUT THE AUTHOR

Tom Larmore has had a very interesting life but can't tell you any of it because of attorney/client privilege. However, he does have three children (grown) and once had two dogs and three cats. He started writing in elementary school when he started his own student newspaper. Dave and Georgia and Other Stories is his first published book.

CPSIA information can be obtained
at www.ICGtesting.com
Printed in the USA
BVHW091944080223
658147BV00011B/144

9 798822 900509